T0063253

Ironblood

Ironblood

WOLF HUNT

KATHERINE A. NEVITT

authorHOUSE®

AuthorHouse™ UK Ltd.
1663 Liberty Drive
Bloomington, IN 47403 USA
www.authorhouse.co.uk
Phone: 0800.197.4150

© 2014 Katherine A. Nevitt. All rights reserved.

No part of this book may be reproduced, stored in
a retrieval system, or transmitted by any means
without the written permission of the author.

Published by AuthorHouse 08/05/2014

ISBN: 978-1-4969-8882-9 (sc)
ISBN: 978-1-4969-8883-6 (e)

Any people depicted in stock imagery provided by Thinkstock are models,
and such images are being used for illustrative purposes only.
Certain stock imagery © Thinkstock.

This book is printed on acid-free paper.

Because of the dynamic nature of the Internet, any web addresses or
links contained in this book may have changed since publication and
may no longer be valid. The views expressed in this work are solely those
of the author and do not necessarily reflect the views of the publisher,
and the publisher hereby disclaims any responsibility for them.

Blood is thicker than water but we need both to survive.

Katherine A Nevitt

Dedicated to

Karl Nevitt,

The father who supports without judgement, the man whose love and care brought about creativity and passion.

Contents

The Hunt

As the dusk light faded into blackness the villagers of Piearre began to tuck themselves away. Children were called inside, shutters were closed on the windows of the wooden cabins, and doors were locked and bolted. The main gate of the village was lowered as guards lit their candles ready for the long night's watch. The cry of a child and the howl of a dog came from somewhere inside the village. On the outside of the gate, shivering and cold was a group of seven men. Wrapped in dense fur coats and trousers made of thick leather they carried a whole army of weapons as they sprinted down the path toward the redwood trees that surrounded the village. Snow crunched beneath their feet. The sobbing of a woman could be heard from inside the walls of the village but not one of them looked back. They kept their eyes fixed on the path ahead with a look of determination plastered on their faces.

Among the men, stood the youngest of them all; a boy of barely eighteen with an unscarred face and innocent mahogany eyes he was the most handsome of them all. The dark hair that usually reached the line of his jaw was pinned back under his heavy furred hood. A woollen scarf wrapped around his nose and mouth protected his face from the bitter cold. His hand shook as he clasped the bow; his father had hand crafted for him, close to his side. He could feel the uneasy movement of his arrow sheathe on his back as he stumbled about on the uneven terrain. He was breathing heavily; not just from the walk but from the feeling of nervousness that welled up inside his stomach. The skin around his eyes already felt frozen.

Feeling a hand on his shoulder, he turned to see a larger boy walking beside him. Being the boy's older brother he was much the same only broader and carrying the scars of many fights and battles. There was a spark in his eye and if his face hadn't been covered a huge smile would have been showing.

"Don't be so nervous," his voice was deep and filled with humour, "It'll be a quick death."

"Don't scare the lad." One of the older men, a short fellow with grey beard hair sticking out from under his protective scarf, shoved the older boy with his elbow.

As they reached the edge of the forest a loud howling sound erupted from somewhere in the distance. Unlike the howling of a dog this howl was cold and wild. It was the howl of the very animal they had been sent out to capture and kill. It was a sound that had the villagers hiding in their cabins, waiting and praying for the first light of dawn. Some of the men seemed to go rigid as they heard the noise others cheered and pounded the air with a glove clad fist.

The leader of the group, a tall well-muscled man with broad shoulders and a scar across his left cheek, turned and raised the torch he'd been carrying. The flame flickered across the faces of the men before him. They were a strong bunch of men. Like a well-oiled machine they fit in together perfectly. They had hunted many times together, surviving only by trusting one and other.

The youngster felt completely out of place next to the seasoned hunters that stood all around him. They made him feel small and insignificant. He felt like curling up in a ball and pretending that he didn't exist. This was not where he wanted to be at all. He longed to be at the top of the village wall, watching from a safe distance.

"Tonight we follow a tradition that has been passed down from generation to generation," The leader's voice rang out loud and true as he began his speech, "Tonight is the night when a boy becomes a man." The group began to cheer and whistle as the leader raised his hand gesturing to the youngest to move forward.

"Tonight is the night when Jed Stoneshield joins his first hunt," he placed his hand on the boy's shoulder and added, "Tonight Jed becomes a man his family can be proud of." One man began to cheer louder than the rest. Jed looked through the crowd and saw his father battering the air with his fist. He was a tall broad shouldered man with many scars to show from his previous hunts. Jed remembered all the stories of near misses and broken bones that his father had told him ever since he was old enough to understand. He felt a wave of nausea course through his body as he wondered what would happen once they entered the forest. He imagined how disappointed his father would be if anything went wrong. Then he thought of his mother and how she'd begged for him to stay inside the village. He remembered how his father had dragged him from her embrace and led him out of the door. He imagined never entering that door again and it took all his effort not to turn and run back to the village. He knew that even if he did they would not open the gate for him. He would have to wait until dawn to gain entry back into the village.

"Let's get on with it." A grumpy voice came from the back of the group. The man that had spoken was a grey haired, elderly man. His hands were beginning to seize up with arthritis and many thought he was too old to join the hunts but he seemed determined to continue until he could go on no more. The others began to nod in agreement with him. The leader raised his hands to calm them and continued to speak,

"Tonight is Jed's time to shine. He will make the first kill. After that you're free to kill as much as you want."

With that he turned and gestured them forward with a flick of his hand. Jed felt his heart skip a beat as he began to follow the rest of the group into the trees. The trunks seemed to loom over him with branches like grabbing fingers. As they headed deeper the snow began to lie less thickly as the trees grew thicker giving more protection to the forest floor. Even protected from the wind by the close growing trees Jed felt chilled to the bone as he imagined what lay ahead. Glancing over his shoulder he saw the trees closing in, hiding the path and what seemed to be the only exit. He gulped down his fear as he turned to look back at the path ahead of him. To his dismay the path had disappeared and beneath his feet was nothing but sludge and leaf mould.

Howling erupted yet again. The men stopped dead in their tracks. Jed found himself almost touching his nose to the back of man in front of him. He stumbled backward so not to barge into him. Lord Edgar, the leader, raised a hand above his head to gesture for complete silence. Jed looked over the man's shoulder and his breath caught in his throat. Movement on the other side of a clearing had him hold his tongue. A shiver of fear sparked at the back of his neck, running down his spine, sending every hair standing on end. A blood thirsty howl raised into the air as a huge black creature launched out of the bushes. It raised its mighty head and howled once again before throwing itself at Lord Edgar. Instantly the group charged into action. Jed stood frozen as he watched the group pounce at the wolf who had knocked Lord Edgar to the ground. The man used the stick of his torch to brace the wolf's chest so that its jaws snapped just above his head. The effort of holding of the wolf could be seen in the tense contours of his face.

The sound of movement behind Jed made him jump. He spun on his heels just quickly enough to see something move out of the corner of his eye.

"There's more coming!" a loud cry was cut off as two more wolves shot from the darkness, circling the group with hunger filled eyes and saliva dripping from their parted jaws.

They looked hungry and ready for blood, their eyes glinting in the darkness.

Without realising it Jed found himself reaching for an arrow over his shoulder. He placed it against his bow and pulled back the string. Just in time he released the arrow as a huge brown monster of a wolf sailed toward him. The wolf seemed to barely feel the arrow that sliced a wound into its left shoulder. It continued toward Jed without halting for a second. Jed's mouth dropped open and his feet froze firmly to the ground as the huge creature landed on top of him. He screamed in utter shock as he was knocked down on the frozen ground. His hand released his bow and he found himself gripping at the creature's neck, trying to hold it off. It was too strong. Its jaws snapped close to his ear. The noise of teeth clashing together was enough to make his whole body quake. He thought of his brother's joke; of how he'd laughed about a quick death. Now he knew his brother had been right. Soon enough he would feel the creature's jaws around his throat and it would all be over.

In a split second he decided that wasn't how it was going to end. Bracing one arm to take the weight of the huge animal, he reached out with his other hand, feeling for something, anything that might help him. His fingers stung as they grazed over something sharp. Grabbing the item he ignored how it sliced into the palm of his hand. Instead he brought it down against the side of the wolf's head. The wolf yelped in pain as blood splattered the forest floor. It toppled to the side, giving Jed chance to roll away from its massive claws as it thrashed in the leaf mould. Looking down at the item in his hand he saw that it was a stone, weather sharpened around its edges. He placed it in his pocket feeling the sentimental value as he realised it had just saved his life. While the wolf was still writhing on the floor he grabbed his bow and readied another arrow. Just about to let it loose in the wolf's chest, he froze as he heard a caterwaul from the other side of the clearing. The first wolf to have attacked had pulled away from Lord Edgar and was backing away into the trees. The other two seemed to change face as they realised what their leader was doing.

"They're retreating." Lord Edgar gasped in shock. Jed watched in astonishment as he realised that he was right. The two wolves that had joined the fray turned and rushed toward the black wolf who turned to head into the trees.

"Don't let them get away!" Gilly, Jed's brother yelled. He charged forward, releasing a spear from his hand. The weapon flew through the air with a striking accuracy and pierced the back of the black wolf. Blood burst from the wound, splattering onto the bare branches of the trees around it. The creature's howl turned to a blood filled gargle as it collapsed in a heap. The other two wolves barely glanced over their shoulders as their companion went down.

The men erupted into cheers as Gilly rushed forward and retrieved the spear from the wolf's back. Bending down, he took a knife from his belt and slit the wolf's throat, allowing it a quick death. Jed watched in horror as blood pooled around the magnificent creature's head, soaking into its jet black fur. Gilly placed a foot on the wolf's back and kicked it onto its side before raising his dagger into the air and cheering triumphantly.

Jed felt a pat on his back and turned to see his father looking down at him proudly. He had removed his scarf as though he was too hot and Jed was shocked to see him smiling.

"You did well." He praised as he dragged his son in for a brief embrace.

"But I didn't get the first kill?" Jed protested.

"It isn't often that a wolf retreats. I got to see my boy fight of a wolf. I can be proud of that." Jed felt his nausea return. *What a gruesome thing to be proud of,* he thought to himself as his father turned and headed over to the other men who had gathered around their first kill. Jed watched him go, wanting nothing more than to turn and head back to the village.

A Brutal Attack

Running through the forest the wolf barely noticed the deer that sprang away in fear as she hurtled toward the mountainside. Her paw pads were red and swollen with the force of her speed. Sludge and mud slowed her, threatening to make her trip with every paw step. The familiar scent of her pack enveloped her as she crossed the boundary line of their territory. Leaving the forest, the snow grew thick and she found herself belly deep in white powder. Releasing a howl she waited for a reply. When it came she knew that the others were waiting for her. A sense of urgency filled the reply making her fur stand on end.

As she hit the mountainside the terrain turned even more slippery and she fought to keep on her paws. The first light of dawn began to spark on the horizon above her head. The snow began to turn of mush as she reached the opening of a cave in the side of the mountain. A strong scent of wolf hit her nostrils. The fur began to lie flat on her shoulders. As she headed into the mountain through a tunnel that pressed in against her flanks another scent hit her nose. She froze and raised her nose to the breeze that drifted from ahead. Her fur began to prickle and her paws tingled as they carried her forward. The iron scent of blood was thick on the air.

She skidded to a halt as the tunnel opened out into a large cavern lit by sunlight that glittered down on the damp walls from a crack in the ceiling. At the back of the cavern two more tunnels broke off into darkness. The cavern was filled with humans. They were all centred in the middle of the cavern, sat on boulders or pacing back and forth. In the middle of the group crouched a young man with long golden hair that reached his shoulders. He held his left elbow with his right hand as though his arm was too heavy for his shoulder. The wolf stood for a moment and shook her head as though clearing bees from her ears. Then within seconds in her place stood a beautiful, pale female with jet black hair that brushed the bottom of her buttocks. She wore trousers and made of leather and a shirt made of spun cotton.

As she stepped forward the crowd around him began to part and the girl stood before him, looking at the wound that sliced across his shoulder. "What happened?" she demanded as she looked around, searching the crowd for the familiar face of her father. He was nowhere to be seen.

"Where is my father?" she demanded, "Where is our leader?" she felt as though everybody were ignoring her as they turned their heads away, each determined not to be the bearer of bad news.

"Baccara, dear," a soothing voice came from the back of the cavern and the crowd parted to allow a beautiful golden haired woman with flecks of grey in her eyes move forward.

"Don't call me that!" the girl spat, "You only ever call me that when something's wrong." Even she felt the sting of her tongue as she saw her mother flinch.

"I'm afraid something's happened." Her mother still spoke in the same smooth voice as she stepped forward and placed a slender fingered hand on her shoulder.

"Then tell me," Cara demanded, "What's happened?" she could feel the crowd moving awkwardly around her, kicking the dusty floor with their toes, looking at the ground.

"It's your father," her mother looked deep into her eyes as she added her free hand to Cara's other shoulder, "He was killed during the night." Cara fell backward, her legs unable to hold her. She felt arms wrap around her and sunk into the chest of the man who had grabbed her. She gazed up at her uncle as he raised her into his lap and she began to weep onto his chest.

After a few moments of sobbing she suddenly burst to her feet again. "Why are you not dead?" she demanded turning to the injured man, "Were you not with him?"

"Cara, Thorn was not the only one with him." Her mother explained as she glanced at Luna a silvery blonde girl with bright green animal like eyes.

"Eva, please don't drag Luna into this. She is just a cub. I am the one to blame. Cara is right. I should have protected out leader better." Thorn spoke in a low tone, looking at the ground at Cara's feet as though he couldn't bare to look her in the eye. Cara threw herself at him ripping at his clothes with her fingers, pounding on his chest with her fists. He remained as still as a brick wall unable and unwilling to fight back. Her uncle Alder grabbed her around the chest and pulled her backward. The tears streamed down her face in an uncontrollable torrent. Alder was a broad shouldered, black haired man with a scarred face. He was a younger version of his brother.

"Cara I promise you I will not rest until the man who did this to your father is dead." Thorn spoke with such force as he pushed himself to his feet and stared her in the face.

"That will not bring my father back!" she screamed at him, "He's gone and there's nothing you can do!" she saw the hurt in his eyes but she didn't care. All she wanted to do was scream and shout. She wanted to release the pain that welled up inside her heart, seeping into her stomach making her feel nauseous.

"None of this can be blamed on Thorn. This is the fault of the humans," Alder told her as he turned her to face him, holding her arms at her sides so that she could not lash out at him, "We will do everything we can to stop these cruel killings but we have to be patient."

"How can you talk like that? He was your brother! He's dead because his packmates couldn't protect him!" she snarled at her uncle, pulling herself away from him. He didn't fight to keep hold of her. Instead he sighed as he threw his hands to his sides.

"Baccara, Alder is pack leader now we must do as he says." Eva explained as she went to take hold of her daughter's hand.

Cara ignored her mother, pulling her hand out of reach, and turned on Thorn again as a thought erupted in her mind, "Where is his body?" she demanded. Thorn gulped as though he were suddenly frightened and trying to hide it.

"We went back to the clearing but the humans had taken it." Thorn explained.

"So not only did you not protect him but you couldn't even bring his body back for the burial he deserves?" she snarled at him. She felt rage and sorrow mix like two chemicals in her stomach that threatened to blow from within.

Feeling as though she might burst into flames with emotion, she suddenly turned on her heels and barged through the group. She felt a hand grab at her arm but she pulled away and continued for the entrance to the cavern. Half way through the tunnel she dropped into a crouch and transformed back into her wolf form. The white flash across her left shoulder sparked as she hit the light outside. Her paws carried her down the mountainside with her mind barely registering where she was headed. She had only one thing on her mind; her father.

Her paws skidded on sludge and she halted as a familiar scent wafted into her nostrils. Dropping her nose to the floor she took in the scent of her father. Following the scent she found herself being led into a large clearing surrounded by moss covered trees. Her heart clenched as she found that in the middle was a large patch of dried blood that had stained into the leaf mould. Even without sniffing she knew who's blood it was. With a whimper, she crouched down on the ground beside the stain and imagined her father's body curled around hers. She imagined the feel of his fur brushing hers. She could even hear his voice in her ear telling her everything was going to be ok. As she broke down crying she found herself transforming once again until she was a girl lay on the ground with her knees pulled up to her chest. Her jet black hair splayed out across the ground, covered her face as her tears soaked into the mud beneath her.

The sound of footsteps made her look up. She turned her head in the direction she'd come from just in time to see a young, fiery haired girl enter the clearing. Her freckled face was twisted in an expression of sympathy.

"Cara, I'm so sorry." Her voice was so full of sympathy that it pulled at Cara's heart. A fresh wave of tears erupted from her eyes, so much so that her vision blurred. The girl crouched beside her and wrapped her arms around her, stroking her back.

"Ivy, how could this happen?" she sobbed into the girl's shoulder. At any other time the feel of her best friend's arms around her would have soothed her but right now they only made her worse. They brought the emotions to the surface as though they were drawing them out of her. She found herself sobbing so much that she was out of breath with the effort.

"I know it's hard," Ivy spoke gently, "We will all miss Gelder. He was a great leader."

"But he was my father!" Cara screamed, "He was the only one who understood me. He was the only one who didn't think I was reckless and stupid." Cara felt hopeless. She had never been a crier. She had never let anybody see her cry. Now she lay bare everything as she imagined a life without her father. The shock of it all sent everything soaring to the surface.

"Cara this isn't helping," Ivy stroked Cara's hair away from her face, "We shouldn't be here. We're too close to the village." Cara could feel how tense her friend was but she didn't care. She couldn't care less if a horde of humans appeared right there and then and killed her where she sat. *At least then I'd be with him,* she thought.

"Cara we have to get out of here. If were caught they'll know were not villagers. They keep track of everyone in and out of these woods. They'll know something's up." Ivy's words dawned on Cara and she stood. Turning on her friend she asked,

"Why should I care? We're all animals to them. They will hunt us down and kill us anyway."

"Don't think like that, Cara. Some of the pack members have been talking about a new life, one living alongside the humans," Ivy explained gesturing toward the village, "All we have to do is wait it out."

"Wait it out until what? Until there are so little left of us that we have to crawl to them for help?" Cara could no longer listen to her friends words. She turned and charged off into the trees.

Relieved not to hear her friend's footsteps behind her she continued onward until she found a shallow gully that had been protected by the roots of a tree and was relatively dry. She settled down in the gully feeling bone tired.

Cara must have nodded off for when she woke she heard the sound of screaming. Jumping to her feet, she was instantly alert, her senses as sharp as her wolf form. Lifting her nose she sniffed the air. Her skin prickled as she recognised the scent of Ivy and underneath it the fresh scent of human. Praying that it wasn't Ivy who had screamed, she leapt out of the gully and began to head back toward the clearing where she'd left her best friend. Her tracing her steps she found she'd gone much further than she thought. With that considered it didn't take her long to return to the clearing for fear of her friend's safety.

Her senses told her to stop just outside the clearing. As she did there was another scream. Her fears were answered. She peered through the bushes into the clearing, careful not to move any foliage or made a sound, and saw Ivy being held by two huge men. Each of them held one of her arms, stretching her out to the point of her chest looking as though it was going to burst open. One of them used his other hand to pull her head back by her hair, forcing her to look up into the eyes of the man who stood before her. He was a tall, well-muscled man wearing the thick brown fur of a wolf he'd clearly killed long ago. The whole idea of wearing wolf skin made Cara's skin crawl. She imagined what they might be doing to her father's pelt as she stood there. She couldn't see his face but she imagined him to be an ugly man with a gruesome expression. With a sick feeling Cara saw that Ivy's face was already bruised and bleeding.

"Where do you come from girl?" the man demanded. He flicked the whip he held in his left hand making it crackle against the floor, sending dead leaves scattering into the air. A draft of air rustled the leaves of the bushes where Cara was hiding. She held her breath as she waited for Ivy to speak. Ivy held her tongue. Cara could see the look of utter defiance and determination on her face, even beneath all the blood and bruises. Cara felt her heart burn with the urge to help her friend. The rage inside her forced a transformation and there was nothing she could do to stop it. Hearing the crackling branches around her, the men turned to look in her direction. She burst through the bushes without even meaning to. Charging into the clearing, she threw herself at one of the men who held Ivy. He released her instantly and fell backward. Leaving him to flounder on the floor she turned to knock the other guard down. Before she could do anything she howled in pain. The whip cracked across her back stinging like a thousand scorpions were piercing her back. She felt a trickle of blood ooze into the fur on her back and wondered just how much damage the whip had done. Her vision turned red with pain and rage as she turned on the man who had struck her. She growled angrily as she heard Ivy pulling herself away from the second man. There was a loud thud as Ivy managed to punch him in the face, almost breaking his nose. The man stumbled backward, shocked at the strength of such a small girl. *Run,* Cara urged her friend.

She was dismayed when she felt the human form of her best friend brush up against her. She had turned to face the third man beside her. *What are you doing you fool?* Cara thought as her friend glared at the man.

"Siding with a wolf?" the man sounded just as shocked as Cara felt, "You're as mad as the village idiot." The man lifted his whip and aimed it for Ivy. Knowing that her thick wolf skin would fair better against the lashing, Cara threw herself in front of Ivy. She pushed Ivy out of the way with her tail, praying that she would take the hint and leave. She felt pain on the tip of her ear as the whip lashed past just missing her eye. Turning, she head butted Ivy on the led, urging her to run.

Finally Ivy's legs began to move. Frustrated with how slow Ivy's human form carried her, Cara forced her head between her legs and flipped her onto her back. Ivy's fingers met in the fur on Cara's neck and she began to race through the forest with her clamped to her back. She could hear the men shouting behind her but didn't look back for fear of slowing. Her back stung as Ivy wriggled on the wound created by the whip. Cara ignored the pain more interested in getting her friend out of danger.

She didn't stop until she was half way up the mountainside and could run no longer. A wave of relief hit her as she collapsed onto the ground, her aching muscles giving a sigh as she allowed them to rest. Ivy climbed off her and collapsed beside her. Changing back to her human form, Cara panted heavily, trying to catch her breath.

"Are you ok?" Ivy asked as she moved closer to Cara and glanced over her shoulder. Cara saw her eyes grow round and spark with shock and fear. Instantly she knew what was wrong. She felt the sting in her back where the whip had sliced her skin. She felt the blood dripping down her back.

"We need to get you back to the den." Ivy grabbed hold of Cara's arm and pulled her to her feet. Cara bit her tongue and winced in pain as the movement caused pain to course through her body, burning in her veins.

They finally stumbled through the tunnel as dusk fell. They were much slower in there human forms and would have managed the hike better in their wolf forms but Cara had been too weak to change. Instead she found herself leaning, clinging desperately to Ivy as pain racked her body. The scent of blood brought the rest of the pack into the main cavern. They looked like scared animals as they cowered at the edge of the cavern, around the tunnel entrances, wondering what was going on. Alder appeared from one of the tunnels. His eyes grew round with shock as he saw the state of the two bruised and battered girls.

"Reach a healer." He ordered the closest pack member who happened to be Luna. She disappeared into the second tunnel without a word like a silver shadow.

Alder rushed over to the two girls and grabbed Cara from Ivy just as she looked like she was about to drop her.

"What the hell happened?" he demanded as he lifted her into his arms and moved her over to a large ledge that came out from the side of the cavern to the left. She winced in pain as he lay her on her side, careful not to touch the open slash on her back.

"She saved my life." Ivy spoke in a voice weak from hunger and thirst. Cara tried to speak but she was too weak. Her body felt as though it was shutting down, protecting itself from all the shock of the day.

"I got to close to the village and some guards caught me," Ivy explained. Cara wanted to protest at her explanation. She couldn't stand the thought of her friend taking all the blame but she was just too weak, "Cara fought them off and took all the beating." Ivy looked down at her feet as though she was ashamed to admit such a thing.

"What form were you in?" Alder demanded. Ivy's head shot up and she flashed a glance at Cara before looking back at him.

"I was in human form." She explained. Alder saw the hesitation in her and hissed,

"What form was Cara in?" he flicked his hand in her direction but never took his eyes off Ivy. Cara felt sympathy for her friend.

"She was in wolf form." Ivy could no longer look him in the eye and she dropped her gaze back to the floor.

A growl erupted deep in Alder's throat as Eva appeared from the tunnel, followed closely behind by Luna.

"Where is she?" Eva demanded. Alder didn't say a word as he moved to allow her a view of her daughter. Eva yelped in shock as she saw the crippled figure that was her daughter.

"I'm going to need poppy seeds and water." Eva explained to Luna who was milling close by. The girl nodded and quickly disappeared out of the cavern into one of the other tunnels.

"Won't she heal on her own?" Ivy asked, looking worried. Eva shook her head and replied,

"Wounds these bad will need a little encouraging."

After a few moments she added, "Ivy, get me some Marigold and blood. I'll need bandages too." Eva barked the orders.

"There's no need," Cara sighed trying to sit up, "I'll heal soon enough." Eva forced her back down, sending a charge of pain shooting through Cara.

"You will not move until I tell you." Eva snarled at her daughter. Seeing that she was in no mood to listen to a word she said, Cara obeyed and lay still.

It wasn't long before the two girls returned with the supplies Eva had asked for.

"Crush the poppy seeds. The powder will send her to sleep while I clean her up." Eva explained. The two girls began to work together to crush the seeds using a few stones they found at the edge of the cavern. Eva leaned forward and began separating Cara's shirt from where it had stuck to her skin with dried blood. Cara winced but held her tongue. Her mother ripped the shirt from her back and picked up the pot of water that Luna had collected. Searing pain scored through Cara as her mother poured the water onto her wound. She gritted her teeth against the pain.

"Here, breathe this in." Luna told her as she held up a handful of crushed poppies to Cara's nose. Cara tried to fight against it for a few moments but before long she felt the powder beginning to work and her vision began to blur. The pain began to dissolve and she found herself drifting into a fitful sleep. The last thing she remembered was the voices of her pack mates all around her.

Intruder

Cara woke to mumbling sound of murmuring voices. The pain in her back had dulled to an ache. She clenched her teeth as she pushed herself into a sitting position. Blinking sleep from her eyes she looked around the cavern. Alder was stood in the middle of the cave. Around him were members of the pack, murmuring and chattering among themselves, looking anxious. Swinging her legs down from the ledge, Cara wobbled to her feet and headed over to the crowd.

"What's going on?" she whispered to Ivy who was crouched at the back of the group. Ivy looked over her shoulder, looking shocked to see Cara stood behind her.

"Alder is setting border patrols. There's been a lot of activity in the forest since we were caught by those stupid humans." She spat with disgust as she spoke, "They attacked Luna last night."

Cara's skin crawled as she heard the words. She shook her head feeling disorientated.

"How long have I been out?" she asked, pressing her hand to her forehead.

"Only a day; Eva said you wounds were healed but your body needed time to recover from the shock." Ivy explained, pressing her palm to Cara's elbow.

"Is Luna ok?" Cara asked, glancing around the cave, trying to set eyes on the silver haired girl.

"She's fine. She's being patched up in Eva's cave. She only got a few bumps and scrapes." Ivy explained flicking her head in the direction of Eva's cave where she did most of her healing.

"Enough talking!" Alder suddenly shouted about the murmur of voices. Everyone fell instantly quiet. Cara pushed her way through the crowd to stand in front of her uncle.

"I'll lead a patrol." She told him, holding her shoulders high and staring him directly in the eye. She prayed he would not object. He grabbed her shoulder and turned her so that he could examine her back.

"How are you feeling?" he asked. He turned her back to him and examined her further.

"I feel fine. I just need to get my claws into something." She told him, "I'll take a border patrol and we can bring back some fresh kill while we're at it." Alder looked surprised at her eagerness.

"Fine. You can lead a patrol up the mountain," Alder replied. Cara was shocked at his reaction. She hadn't expected him to even let her out of the cave, "There's been sightings of the Greytooth pack up there."

"But I thought we were supposed to be patrolling the forest?" Cara objected. Alder shook his head and replied,

"I'll lead a forest patrol. I don't want you anywhere near the village at the moment." Cara was about to protest when he raised an eyebrow, almost daring her to speak against him. Instead she sighed and turned to look at the group in front of her.

"I'll take Ivy and Fang with me." She told her leader. He nodded and glanced over the crowd himself.

"Take Wren with you too," he flicked his finger at a small pale faced, brown haired girl of only fifteen. She fiddled with the seam of her top as she heard her name being called. Cara sighed feeling as though she was being put on babysitting duty. Instead of arguing, she turned to Fang, a tall broad shouldered nineteen year old. A scar crossed his right eye reminding Cara of the stories she'd heard when she was a pup. Fang's parents had been murdered by humans while he'd hidden in the bushes close by. Seeing the faded lump of scar tissue on his face every time she looked at him she felt her heart bleed for her pack member.

She gestured for him to follow her and pushed her way through the crowd. Ivy was already waiting at the entrance of the cavern. She was kicking the dusty floor with her toes as though she was eager to leave.

"Wren, come on!" Cara shouted to the pale faced girl as she headed for the entrance. The girl scuttled across the cave and followed her through the tunnel.

The patrol headed up the mountainside in wolf form. Cara welcomed the feel of the wind rushing through her fur as she sped through tall grass, pouncing over fallen trees and boulders. She heard the speeding paw steps of her pack mates behind her and felt a rush of exhilaration. Lifting her nose she scented the air. As they reached the top of the mountain, she stopped dead. Glancing over her shoulder she shot a thought toward Ivy, *Do you smell that?* The ginger wolf lifted her nose and instantly nodded.

Greytooth pack, Fang agreed. He bared his teeth and began to sneer. Cara glanced around her, still sniffing the air. The scent of unfamiliar wolves washed over her and made her fur stand on end. Out of instinct she began to bare her own teeth.

Something moved on the mountainside in front of her. Zoning her eyes in on the movement, a low growl escaped her throat.

Intruders, she snarled.

Bacara! Wait! Fang blasted the thought at her as she began to charge down the mountainside. He was too late. Instead of listening to him she continued at a true speed. Crashing through the bushes, she ran in the direction of the movement. Throwing herself into a clearing, she skidded to a halt and glared at the intruder. The huge speckled grey wolf turned in her direction, baring its teeth that were covered in crimson blood. The rabbit that lay at its feet still twitched with the distant signs of life.

Your hunting on Ironblood territory, she snarled as she braced herself ready to pounce at the intruder. She felt fur brush up against her side and knew that the members of her pack had joined her.

Food is scarce. I will hunt where I like, the wolf retorted, turning back to his kill and gripping it in his wide jaws. Cara felt her haunches rise on the back of her neck as she watched the wolf turn and disappear into the bushes.

We should get back and report this to Alder, Wren's thoughts were full of fear and Cara wanted to turn on her and bite her tail to let her know just what it felt like in the real world.

We don't need Alder to sort this, she snarled at her pack mate and began to follow the scent of the strange wolf.

Before long she came across him crouched beneath the huge branches of an ancient redwood tree. The sound of bone crunching hit her ears as he chewed on the rabbit still warm body.

That prey belongs to the Ironblood pack, she glared at him with ice blue eyes that were ablaze with anger.

And what's a pretty little wolf like you going to do about it? The wolf looked up from his meal, glaring at her in defiance. Without another word Cara flung herself at the wolf with a loud howl of anger. She felt her teeth meet in fur as she landed on top of him. He squealed in surprise and jumped to his paws, trying to shake her off. Gripping on with her strong jaws, she raked her claws across his back.

A chorus of howling rose up into the air as the members of her pack appeared behind her. Ivy was the first to join the fight. She lunged at the wolf's paws, biting and nipping at his legs, trying to tip him over. It worked well and he soon toppled. Cara leapt from his back just before he rolled, knowing he would crush her with his weight. She stepped up onto his chest, and pinned him to the floor, glaring deep into his brown flecked eyes.

Get out of Ironblood territory and stay out or we'll use your fur to line our beds, she snapped her jaws close to his ear, warning him.

Feeling him tense with fear beneath her, she waited a few moments before releasing him. As he jumped to his paws and began to run for his own territory at the bottom of the mountain, Ivy snapped at his tail, giving him one last warning bite before watching him disappear with a look of satisfaction smearing the fur on her face.

Let's get back to the cave and report this, Fang suggested. Cara finally nodded. She glanced over her shoulder as the others began to head back to the top of the mountain. She could see the bushes rustling further down the mountain as the wolf headed to the river beyond.

Reaching the cave entrance, Cara glanced over her shoulder to see Ivy and the others dropping down onto the ledge behind her. They all looked ruffled with the effort of the journey home. Wren was panting heavily and had struggled to keep up the whole way home. Cara rolled her eyes with frustration as she saw the she-wolf drop down to rest.

Pushing her way through the tunnel into the cavern, she raised her nose, scenting for her other pack mates. The scent of Alder was faint and she guessed he had not yet returned from his own patrol. She shook herself, transforming into her human state. On the far side of the cavern Eva appeared from her the tunnel that led to her own den. Her eyes sparked with shock when she saw Cara stood before her.

"Alder told me you took a patrol out." Eva spoke in a calm voice as she began to pick up the pile of herbs that lay scattered on the cave floor at the entrance of the tunnel.

"Yes, we caught a Greytooth on pack territory." Cara explained to her mother. Eva's head whipped up and she began to examine Cara from her to toe very quickly.

"Are you hurt again?" she demanded as she rushed to her daughter's side, sniffing the air as if she expected the scent of blood. Cara shook her head.

"I can't say the same for the intruder." She felt a giggle of satisfaction bubbling up inside her. Eva's shoulders loosened and she went back to her work.

"Where is everyone?" Cara asked. The cavern felt emptier than usual. The scent of Luna came from the tunnel behind her mother but everyone else's scents were faded as though they hadn't been there for a while.

"Everyone is either out on patrol or hunting." Her mother explained, "I have work to do." Cara felt the cold strike of her mother's tongue as though she was pushing her away. She watched silently as she disappeared into the tunnel.

The rushing sound of fur on stone made Cara turn just in time to see the large grey form of her uncle stride into the cavern. He shook his broad head and leaves scattered onto the floor. A moment later he stood a tall, muscular man. Cara rushed over to him and immediately began to report what they'd seen on the outskirts of their territory. She felt her blood boiling as she recalled the intruder and his arrogant attitude.

"I think we may have bigger problems than a few other wolves." Alder sighed once she had finished. He brushed gently past her and headed over to sit on the ledge where Cara had recovered from her injuries the night before.

"What do you mean?" Cara asked, joining him quickly as the other members of his patrol began to pour in through the tunnel with Ivy and Fang among them.

"The humans seem to have been putting a lot of silver wire traps down." he explained as he grabbed a blanket made of wool from the back of the ledge. He threw it over himself and placed is head against the rock wall.

"Has anyone been caught in them?" Cara asked, feeling a sick sensation in her stomach as she imagined the damage the wire traps could do to her pack mates. She remembered how one wolf had lost his tail to one and another had nearly died of blood loss. It made her shudder.

Seeing her shaking Alder placed a comforting hand on her shoulder and replied, "Nobody has been caught yet and hopefully never will."

"What are you going to do about it? We can't stay out of the forest. We need the prey it provides." Cara asked, wondering what other dangers the traps could hold for her pack.

"I'm going to send a scout team out in the morning to destroy as many traps as possible." Alder explained, he then flicked his hand gesturing to dismiss her, "Please leave me. I need to rest. It's been a long day." Cara nodded respectfully and turned to head away.

"Cara," he said stopping her in her tracks. She looked over her shoulder and he smiled at her, "I'm sorry about what happened to your father but you should know he would be very proud of you." Cara found tears beading in her eyes and couldn't say another word. Instead she forced a smile and headed away.

Cara prowled through the undergrowth with the sound of paw steps behind her. The early morning sun was shifting above their heads, melting the dew that covered the forest floor. The morning was a fresh one and birds had begun to sing in the trees. Cara felt the oddest sense of peace for the first time in days since her father had been murdered. Being close to the village, she pricked her ears and could hear the sounds of villagers waking. She could hear the sound of window shutters opening and fires being set. Nausea sparked inside her as she imagined the villagers going about their daily business having no idea what they had done to her pack.

Glancing over her shoulder she saw Ivy and Thorn walking side by side. The two kept glancing at each other while the other wasn't looking. It sent a giggle through Cara to see them acting so stupid. Rolling her eyes she flicked her tail, gesturing them to stop and halted. She turned and said,

I'll go ahead on my own. It'll be easier to stay hidden. You two should check by the river, she flicked an ear in the direction of the river that cut through the territory which was the only source of water the pack used. It reached all the way through the mountainside weathering small caves and gorges as it went. Ivy's ears twitched as though she wanted to protest but Thorn was the one who spoke up first,

Alder said not to go off alone.

Do you see him around anywhere? Cara demanded, glancing around, pretending to look for her uncle. She flicked her tail in frustration, *I'm in charge right now and I'm telling you to go to the river.* Thorn lowered his head, unable to look her in the eye.

Sorry, I just don't want anyone else getting hurt.

Nobody will, just go. Cara urged. She longed to be alone for a while. Ivy and Thorn finally bowed their heads before turning and heading off in the other direction.

Once she could no longer hear their footsteps, she turned and headed the other way. All her senses were turned in the direction of the village. When she was close enough to see the gates of the village through the trees, she skidded to a halt, transforming into her human form. She stood, looking at the men who wandered up and down atop the walls of the village. The sounds of children playing and dogs barking came from inside the walls. Cara imagined what it looked like inside. The curiosity of how the other species lived was growing stronger by the day as she imagined what might have happened to her father's body.

Something suddenly moved out of the corner of her eye. She jumped backward in shock. Her leg was jerked from under her and she screamed in pain as she was yanked up into the air. Pain pierced her ankle as she felt metal slice into her skin. She felt blood oozing down her leg. Pulling herself upward she managed to catch a glimpse of the silver wire that looped around her ankle.

The sound of movement startled her again. She looked around trying to determine where the noise was coming from. Her senses felt disorientated as the blood rushed toward her head. Fear spread through her like poison as she saw the bushes move at the edge of the clearing. A man stepped out into the clearing. A cold shiver surged through her. Even upside down Cara could see that he was broad shouldered and muscular beneath the fur and leather of his clothes. His face was covered by a thick fur hood and a woollen scarf. The only feature on his face that Cara could see was his intense mahogany eyes. He stared at her with those eyes and she could see the shock deep within them. Cara found herself struggling to hide her fear as he stepped forward, removing a dagger from his belt. Her sink tingled as he wrapped an arm around her waist. A moment later her leg was released and she found herself kneeling on the ground in front of him. He stepped backward to look at her. She crouched clutching her wounded ankle with her hand. Blood oozed between her fingers. She flinched as he raised a hand to his face. She was shocked when he lowered his hood and removed the scarf from his face. He had long dark brown hair that swept his jawline and sharp cheekbones that gave a masculine look to his young face. He crouched down in front of her and when he spoke his voice was deep and throaty.

"You look scared to see the face of the man who just freed you." He reached for his belt and removed a water skin from it. Removing the cork from it he held it above Cara's ankle and asked, "May I?" speechless all she could do was nod as she removed her hand from her ankle. She winced in pain as he tipped the water onto her wound.

"You know you shouldn't be out here alone," he placed the cork back into the bottle and tied it back to his belt, "It's dangerous in these woods."

"I can take care of myself." Cara snapped, suddenly finding her voice.

"She speaks," he raised his hands as though gesturing a miracle and laughed, "Though her words are stupid. You do not have a weapon to protect yourself with." Cara found herself flinching away from the dagger that he still clasped in his hand. Seeing her fear, he placed the dagger back in its sheathe.

"I won't harm you." He spoke gently. Cara struggled to stop herself from laughing in his face.

She could no longer stand the tension in her body. Jumping to her feet she turned on her heels and began to run.

"Hey wait!" she heard him call from behind her. Footsteps sounded behind her and she knew he was chasing after her. Picking up speed, she charged through the forest, desperate to outrun him.

It didn't take long but it felt like a lifetime. When she realised she could no longer hear him following she skidded to a halt. Panting for breath she leaned over with her hands on her knees. Her heart pounded with the effort of running.

"What's that smell?" Ivy asked as she joined Cara at the edge of the river. Cara sat atop a boulder with her feet dangling into the cold water. Cara raised her nose and sniffed. She shook her head and looked at Ivy with a confused look on her face. Ivy stepped forward. Moving her nose close to Cara she sniffed again. She flinched backward, grimacing, "You stink of human."

"I have no idea what you're talking about." Cara replied, looking away from Ivy, unable to look her in the eye. The truth was she knew exactly what her friend was talking about. Since that morning she could think of nothing else but the kindness of the man who had cut her from the wolf trap. Questions filled her mind as she wondered why he'd helped her.

"Have you been attacked again?" Ivy asked, "Are you hurt?" Cara sighed as she realised her friend wasn't going to give up asking questions. She shook her head and turned to look at her friend.

"Can I trust you?" she asked, glancing around her, listening for any sign of other pack members that might be close by. Ivy looked at her with an angry expression on her face.

"Of course you can trust me! I'm your best friend." Ivy hissed at her as she slapped Cara roughly on the shoulder. Cara took a deep breath as she slipped off the boulder into the icy water of the river. She had to remove the smell of the human from her skin. Ivy stared at her in astonishment.

"What are you doing?" she gasped as she watched Cara dunk her head under the water.

"I need to get rid of his scent." Cara told her friend as her head burst above the surface of the water. Ivy dropped onto her knees at the edge of the water and stared at Cara.

"Who? What the hell are you talking about?" Ivy asked. Her face was twisted with a look of confusion and curiosity.

"I got caught in a trap today." Cara explained. Ivy gasped yet again. She looked as though she was examining Cara with a close eye. She looked as though she was about to burst into another stream of questions.

Cara raised her hand to stop her before she could speak. "I was caught in a trap and a human let me go. He cut me free and cleaned my wound." She explained as she climbed out of the water and lifted the hem of her trouser leg that covered the now sealed wound where the trap had cut into her skin. She was relieved that her quick healing had kicked in. Ivy looked gobsmacked as she stared down at the scarring wound.

"He just let you go?" Ivy asked, unable to take her eyes off the wound. Cara shrugged her shoulders and replied,

"Well technically I ran away but he didn't attack me." Ivy shook her head as though she couldn't believe it. Cara was struggling to believe it herself but she'd been there. He really had let her go. It was the only reason she was stood in front of Ivy now.

"But they attack anyone who's outside the village?" Ivy protested.

"Well he didn't ok." Cara yelled at Ivy suddenly feeling defensive. She hated the thought that her friend didn't believe her.

Bitten

Night had fallen. The village was locked up and the gates had been lowered. Jed stood at the top of the village wall. Clasped in his hand he held his bow. He peered over the wall into the forest. He struggled to pick out the figures of the men who had just entered the trees. The sound of a wolf howling sent shivers down his spine as he watched the men disappear. The first howl of the night sounded sending shivers down Jed's back.

"Come back safe." He whispered as he thought of his father and brother who had joined the hunting group. He had chosen to stay behind after going out on the two nights previous. Now he sat guarding the village, praying that no wolves would try to get inside. He couldn't remember the last time a wolf had made it into the village. He only remembered the stories his father had told him when he was a child. Stories that had kept him awake at night thinking he could hear a wolf scratching at the wooden wall beside his bed. The stories still brought a lump to his throat.

Jed jumped as he saw movement at the edge of the forest. His heart stopped as he recognised the figure of a young boy. Anger rose inside him as he made out the slow, stumbled gait of his younger brother, Jasper. After arguing with his father about joining the hunt he'd quickly not listened when he'd been told her had to stay at home. The stupidity of his brother angered him. He had no wish to join in the hunts yet he was forced to do so. He had no idea why his brother would want to join them. It was dangerous and Jasper was stupid for sneaking out to follow them.

Jed suddenly thought of the jagged pieces of rock that stuck out of the village wall and how they reminded him of a stone ladder. He pulled his bow over his head and one shoulder, freeing up his hands. Pulling himself up onto the side of the village wall, he glanced down at the dusty floor below. It was shrouded in shadow and mystery covered with bushes and grass. His heart thudded in his chest as he lowered himself down toward the first foothold.

"Hey kid, what are you doing?" a voice shouted from behind him. He ignored the guard as he lowered himself down. He heard the commotion at the top of the wall but didn't look up. Focusing on where he was putting his feet, he was little more than half way down before his foot slipped. It didn't matter how much he clung to the wall with his hands, the dislodged stone sent him spiralling toward the ground. Dizziness filled him with nausea as he spun toward the ground. Pain seared through him as he hit the ground on his back. The wind was knocked from his lungs and he coughed and gasped for air. Wiggling his toes he was relieved to see he hadn't done too much damage to his back. As he sat up he felt a sharp ache in his spine. The howling of another wolf was like an off switch to his pain and suddenly he was only thinking of his brother. He climbed to his feet and shook the dirt from his clothes. Removing his bow from his back he was relieved to see it was not damaged from the fall. Taking an arrow from the sheathe on his back, he readied his bow before heading down the path toward the forest. Every sense was alert for the signs of danger. Looking at the tracks on the ground he picked out the smallest as his brother's and began to follow them. For the most part they followed the group of hunters. Jed found himself shaking with fear as he realised his brother's tracks had begun to stray from the others. He knew there was nothing worse than being out in the forest alone at night. The thought of his brother meeting trouble was too great. His pace quickened almost without him even realising it.

Soon he was charging through the forest, making enough noise to wake the dead. No longer caring for his own safety he raced through the forest on the heels of his brother. He stopped dead. A low growling came from the other side of the bushes in front of him. With a sickening feeling he realised his brother's tracks led straight in the direction of the sound. Taking one hand off his bow he parted the leaves of the bush to peer through. Just then there was a loud yell of terror. Jed felt his fingertips tingle as he readied his bow again. Pushing through the bush he found his brother splayed out on the ground. On top of him was a huge black wolf with piercing brown eyes. Its jaws were clamped around Jasper's forearm. Blood welled between its teeth. Jasper was screaming in agony. Jed raised his bow to eye level and shot. The arrow sliced through the air making a whistling sound and pierced the wolf's eye with deadly precision. The creature didn't even have time to yelp as the arrow purged its brain. It toppled to the ground, releasing Jasper's arm. The boy clutched his injured arm to his chest with his good hand. He was whimpering like a wounded animal. His short black hair was resting away from his face and Jed could see the bloody scratches on his cheeks.

Moving forward Jed crouched down beside his brother. He rolled the wolf away from them while whispering,

"Be quiet of there'll be another one on us in a few seconds." His brother seemed to bite down on his tongue as he tried desperately to stay quiet. Blood pulsed from his wound, soaking his clothes and Jed could see the fight fading from Jasper's eyes. He grabbed his shirt from under his fur coat and ripped a large strip off. Grabbing Jasper's arm away from him, he bound the wound as tightly as he could. He no longer felt any fear. Pure adrenaline was pulsing through his veins. With strength he had never known he possessed he picked Jasper up and threw him over his shoulder. Holding him tightly he began to head back toward the village, praying they would be allowed back in.

At the gates Jed began to shout and scream, begging for entry. His pleas seemed to fall upon deaf ears. The villagers would not let anyone inside until dawn pierced the velvet night sky.

Giving up he turned to the shelter of the bushes that grew against the village wall. Crouching, he gently laid Jasper onto the grass. The boy was no longer conscious. Loss of blood and shock had sent him into an eye twitching, murmuring state that worried Jed down to his bones. Taking his water skin from his belt he poured some water into Jasper's mouth. Jed was relieved when Jasper managed to drink a little. Taking advantage of his brother's comatose state Jed used the time to examine his brother's wound. He removed the strip of cloth he'd used to bind his brother's wound and gasped at the sheer extent of the damage. Although the wound was no longer bleeding the wolf's teeth had gone right down to the bone. The flesh was punctured in several different places as though the wolf had chomped down again and again. Jed was sickened by the thought of how much pain his little brother was in.

Rebinding his brother's wound he lay down beside him. Feeling how cold his brother had become he pulled him up onto his lap and wrapped himself around his brother. The cold bitter night wind ripped through the bushes chilling him to the bone. He could only imagine how cold his brother was.

Jed must have nodded off for when he woke he could hear the sound clanging metal which signalled the opening of the village gates. He could feel Jasper breathing faintly on top of him and knew how much trouble his brother was in. he moved carefully so not to cause his brother too much pain and lifted him up into his arms. The sound of voices hit his ears sending a surge of hope through him. Pushing his way through the bushes, he saw the gate coming into view. The first light of dawn was glittering on the horizon, shining of the dew that covered the grass. However it was not the dawn that Jed was relieved to see. Stood at the gates, waiting to enter the village was the hunting party. Picking up his pace with his heavy load, Jed rushed toward them. Startled faces turned to look at him. Gasps of horror filled the air as they saw Jasper lay limply in his arms.

Jed's father shouldered his way through the group to stand in front of his sons.

"Jasper no!" he gasped as he rushed forward to take his son from Jed's arms. He held him tightly to him with his head pressed into his son's chest.

"What happened?" Lord Edgar demanded as he joined Jed. His father was already disappearing through the gate, probably on his way to a healer.

"I was guarding the wall. I saw Jasper going into the forest and I knew something bad was going to happen." Jed explained with his eyes turned away from Edgar's face purely out of shame for leaving the village without permission.

"How did you get through the gate?" Edgar demanded. Jed shook his head.

"I didn't. I climbed down the wall." He explained, pointing to the jagged rocks he'd used as foot holds to climb down the wall.

"He should be punished for something so reckless." A voice came from behind Edgar. The lord raised his hand above his shoulder for silence as he looked down at Jed, examining as though he was wondering how to proceed.

"I will deal with you later. Right now we should make sure that your brother is ok." With that Edgar turned and headed inside the village where he was greeted by his wife, Fiona who plastered his face with kisses as she did every time he returned from a hunt.

For some reason Jed found himself wondering if he would ever have a wife who would do such a thing. He shook his head remembering that he should be worrying about his brother not wondering about lovers. Try as he might to forget it he still couldn't get the face of the girl he'd rescued out of his mind. There was something about her that stuck like spikes in his brain.

***

The dawn brought with it melting dew that soaked Cara's fur as she wandered through the forest with Ivy and Wren behind her. Alder had sent them out in search of prey. So far they'd managed to catch two rabbits, barely enough to feed one hungry adult wolf at best. Wren had slowed them with her constant questions on the best hunting techniques. Being the youngest in the pack meant she was always looking for guidance from her older pack mates. Cara found it irritating to say the least. She longed to send her off on her own to find her own prey but knew that she'd only go getting herself into trouble.

The irony scent of blood had Cara stop in her tracks. Ivy bumped into her rear as though she hadn't been expecting to stop so suddenly.

A little warning would be nice, Ivy moaned as she rubbed her sore nose with her paw.

Do you smell that? Cara asked, ignoring her friend's moaning. Ivy lifted her nose and sniffed the air. He eyes grew round with fear as she too smelled what had hit Cara's nose. Wren was silent for the first time during the whole hunt. Cara dropped into a crouch and began to creep forward in the direction of the scent. She flicked her tail indicating for the others to follow her quietly.

Cara gasped at the scene on the other side of the bushes. She heard a whimper come from Ivy and knew she was not seeing things. Slumped in a puddle of its own blood was a huge black wolf. Under the stench of blood was the scent of the Greytooth pack. Cara felt guiltily relieved that this wolf did not carry the scent of her own pack.

Cara, this is bad, Ivy groaned. She had walked around the wolf, inspecting it and had stopped at its head. Her nose was close to its jaws and she was sniffing the crimson liquid that had dried on its yellowed fangs.

This wolf attacked a human, Ivy looked at Cara with worry shining in her green wolf eyes. Cara felt dread welling inside her. The arrow protruding from the wolf's eye clearly showed that the wolf hadn't managed to finish his kill. A shiver raced down Cara's spine.

Take Wren back to the cave and report this to Alder. I'm going to look around some more, Cara told her friend. Ivy tipped her head to one side and looked like she was going to protest. After a few moments she sighed and nodded.

Flicking her tail to Wren she began to lead the way back toward the cave.

When she was sure they were gone she shook off her wolf form in favour of standing on two legs to assess the situation. Even though she had been staring at the body for several minutes, the sight still chilled her to the bone. Flashing images of her father sped through her mind as she wondered if this was how he had died. It brought tears to her eyes and soon she was on her knees. Throat wrenching sobs burst from her chest and she wrapped her arms around herself.

"Hey, what's wrong?" An oddly familiar voice startled her out of her misery. She jumped to her feet, spinning around. A strange fluttering feeling enveloped her stomach as her eyes fell upon the man who had cut her from the silver trap.

"You shouldn't creep up on people like that!" Cara snapped at him, feeling her soaked cheeks burn red. The man threw his arms up in the air as though he was surrendering. It was an odd gesture that had Cara putting her head to one side. She had never met a human who had not wanted to harm her before. Even in human form she had taken many beatings simply for being a stranger too close to the village without good enough reason.

"You're not crying over that thing are you?" He sneered as he flicked a hand to gesture the dead wolf that now lay behind her.

"That thing is a beautiful being that didn't deserve such a brutal death." Cara snapped at him. Deep down she knew she was not talking about the Greytooth wolf. She was talking about her father. She couldn't help thinking about how he must have died. She wanted to throw herself at the human and grip his throat in her teeth.

"That 'beautiful being' tried to kill my brother last night. It got what it deserved." He spat back at her. Cara knew she should be angry at his words but instead they lit a fire of curiosity inside her.

"Tried to?" She echoed. The man nodded and replied in a voice filled with triumph,

"I shot it down before it had chance to go for his throat." Cara felt terror rising inside her. This was worse than she thought.

"Was your brother bitten? Did he survive?" She demanded, taking an urgent step toward him. He looked confused over her questions, raising an eyebrow as he answered,

"He was bitten on the forearm and yes he survived." Cara felt her knees go weak. Before she knew it she was sinking toward the ground. The man sped forward with such speed Cara hadn't known humans to possess and wrapped his arms around her. He held her up as though he was determined not to let her fall.

"This isn't happening." Cara found herself shaking uncontrollably, "this can't be happening."

"What are you talking about?" He held her in a way that he could look at her face. Cara felt mahogany and blue eyes meet for just a second before she forced him away from her.

"You have to take me to him." Cara demanded. The man looked suspicious.

"Take you to who?"

"Your brother. Your whole village could be in danger."

The man didn't get a chance to ask any more questions. Cara whipped around at the sound of heavy, thudding paw-steps. Her heart sank as she saw brown fur through the bushes. The familiar scent of grizzly bear hit her nostrils.

"You need to get out of here now." Cara threw over her shoulder at the man.

"What? Why? What the hell is wrong with you?" He demanded. No matter how Cars tried she couldn't stop it. The pure fear her human form felt in the face of danger was enough for her to turn. She couldn't stop herself. She knew she couldn't defend herself against such a beast in her human form. She winced at the gasp from the human behind her. She prayed it was because of the bear that was ambling toward them but she knew better. She could feel his astonished stare burning into her back as she turned to face the grizzly. It reared up in front of her, roaring loudly. Cara pounced, leaping over the bear's head as it swung huge claws toward her. A yell of pain erupted behind her and she knew the man had taken the blow.

Landing on all fours she knew she should run but as she turned to see the bear looming down on the man she knew she couldn't leave. She remembered how he had cut her from the trap and knew she had to return the favour. The world couldn't do with losing one of the very few kind humans. Taking a deep breath to prepare herself, she charged and leapt onto the bear's back. Gripping its neck with her teeth she bit down as hard as she could. The bitter taste of bear blood oozed between her fangs and she had to fight not to let go. The bear reared up again trying to shake her off. She could hear the man moving in the leaf mould. The sound of a dagger being pulled from its sheathe hit her ears. A few moments later the bear let out a choking sound and she began to topple forward. The man fell back onto his buttocks as Cara leapt down onto the ground in front of him. Steadying herself, she stood motionless, waiting for him to swing his dagger her way.

She was surprised when it never came. Instead the dagger slipped from his hand, onto the ground. He raised the hand toward her, his eyes filled with both curiosity and fear. Cara remained still as his fingertips brushed the fur on her cheek. A spark shot through her as she pressed her cheek into the palm of his hand. She remained still, waiting for him to make another move. When he stayed motionless, she took a deep breath and allowed herself to change. His eyes widened and she heard his sharp intake of breath but he didn't move his hand away. Cara felt her cheek tingling where his fingertips connected with her skin. As she stared at him, wondering when he would finally react she saw his eyes flickering as though he was trying to keep them open. She gasped with shock as she lowered her eyes from his and saw the huge gaping claw marks across his chest. The irony scent of human blood made her nose wrinkle as she leaned forward and peels his coat away from the sticky crimson liquid that oozed from the wounds. She was about to stand up and head into the forest to look for something to bind his wounds with when he grabbed her arm.

"Don't leave me alone." He gasped as his wounds stung with the effort of speaking. Cara felt every bone in her body urging her to move but she couldn't leave him. She saw the pleading in his eyes and knew she couldn't leave his side.

In that split second she made a decision that could change everything forever. She lifted her wrist to her mouth and readied herself for pain as she bit down hard, drawing blood.

"What are you doing?" the man's voice was little more than a whisper as Cara held her wrist over his wounds. Her thick, ruby red blood dripped down onto his wounds. He gasped as though her blood had burned him and his whole body jerked. Cara watched in wonder as she had many times before as his wounds began to knit and heal together. He watched also. She could feel him tensing with curiosity as he watched.

"How the hell did you do that?" he demanded, pulling away from her a little, "What the hell are you?" there was the reaction she'd expected. He jumped to his feet, grabbing his dagger from where it lay on the ground where he'd dropped it. Cara stayed crouched, raising her hands in surrender as he pointed the dagger toward her.

"No need to thank me for saving your life." She sighed sarcastically.

"Don't try and change the subject. What are you?" He demanded, jabbing the dagger toward her chest. His face was twisted into an angry, confused grimace. Cara dodged backward out of the way of the dagger, still holding up her hands.

"I would have thought that was obvious," she shrugged her shoulders as she finally answered him, "I'm a Lycan."

"A werewolf?" His eyes grew wide as he spoke the word. It was as though saying it had helped it to sink in. He no longer looked angry. Instead his mahogany eyes flashed with fear. Cara felt her heart clench. She had no idea why it hurt her to see him scared of her but it did.

Before she could say another word, he charged her, aiming his dagger directly at her heart.

"You're a beast!" He yelled as he stomped forward. Cara raised her hands. He stopped dead as she grabbed his wrist. The tip just barely touched the cotton that covered her skin, piercing a tiny hole. He looked confused for a moment as he looked down at her hands wrapped around his wrist. Then he drove forward with new force. Just as he did Cara twisted taking his wrist with her. Wrapping his arm up against his back she forced it upward until he had no choice but to release the dagger. It clattered to the ground as it bounced on tiny pebbles. Cara whipped him around and forced him back against a tree, bracing an arm across his chest so that he couldn't move.

"As much as I'd love to spend the rest of the day dancing with you we don't have time. Your brother and your whole village are in very real danger." He stopped trying to push free and looked at her. As though he saw the seriousness in her eyes, he stopped fidgeting.

"What danger might that be?" He asked.

"Your brother has been bitten. If you don't take me to him he could die or he may become just like me. A Lycan has venom in their saliva. If a human is bitten and is strong enough to fight the poison they will turn only they can't control their blood lust. That comes from years of practise." Cara explained.

"Is that what happened to you? Were you bitten?" The man's question caught her off guard. She had never had to explain her own existence before. Shaking her head she replied,

"My parents are Lycans. I was born like this," then she realised what was happening. They were veering off track again. "Look I promise to answer all of your questions later. Just get me to your brother before it's too late."

"Ok but I am not taking you anywhere until you tell me your name."

"Baccara." She replied feeling that it was an easy price to pay for his cooperation.

Like the black roses? That's a beautiful name." He smiled at her. She shoved him hard against the tree.

"Stop changing the damn subject." She hissed at him feeling her blood boil. She could feel her fingertips growing long and pointed into claws. Removing her hands from him, she took a deep breath to calm herself and shook her hands.

"My name is Jed in case you were wondering." He shot her a perfectly white smile as he turned and began to head in the direction of the village.

The Climb

Cara stared at the huge stone wall that loomed over her head. She had never been so close to the village before. The wall was the largest most magnificent structure she had ever seen in her life. It was much different from the redwood trees where her pack resided. She was awestruck as she watched Jed climbing the wall. He was more graceful than she'd ever known a human to be. Every movement was sure and steady.

He stopped half way up and looked over his shoulder at her.

"Aren't you coming?" He demanded. Taking a deep, shaky breath, Cara nodded. Climbing mountains and trees to find prey was one thing but to climb a stone wall into what could be her death was another. She raised her foot into the first foothold like she'd seen Jed do. Then gripping tightly, allowing her fingers to grow long claws, she began to pull herself upward. Her claws scrapped against the stone making a sound that made her ears ring. She clenched her teeth against it.

Her heart felt as though it was beating so quickly that it might burst from her chest. It grew worse when she chanced a glance down. Seeing how high she was made her dizzy. She clutched tighter to the rock, pressing herself closely to the wall.

"Come on your nearly at the top." She heard Jed's voice. It was warm and encouraging. She looked up to see that he had pulled himself over the lip of the wall and was looking down at her with a hand outstretched. She pulled herself up a few more metres and reached out for her hand. Her fingertips met his palm but her hand fell short. She suddenly felt her foot slipping from its hold, the rock crumbling beneath her weight. She braced herself ready to fall, closing her eyes tightly knowing that in moments she would hit the ground below with bone breaking force. She was amazed when instead of falling she felt herself being lifted. Her feet dangled beneath her as they were removed from the wall. Jed had grabbed the collar of her shirt and was pulling her upward. Her stomach clenched as she heard the breath-taking sound of material ripping. Just as quickly as she'd been grabbed, she felt herself falling again. A scream escaped her mouth but was cut off as she felt herself stopped short. He'd grabbed her hand and was holding on for dear life. She gripped his hand even more tightly than he had hers. She could see the effort on his face as he began to pull her upward again.

"What's going on over there?" A deep voice called from somewhere behind Jed. Whoever it was had clearly heard her scream. The sound of rushed footsteps came toward them just as Jed pulled her over the lip of the wall. She collapsed onto the stone at his feet. She panted for breath never having felt so breathless in her life. A guard stood over them with a suspicious glare on his face. His hand was clasped on the hilt of the sword at his belt. He was a tall man wearing thick brown padded clothing and a hood to match. He smiled like alcohol.

"My girlfriend thought she'd seen something. She was leaning too far and slipped," Jed explained, "she's fine now. You can go back to your post." The man still looked suspicious. He looked from Jed to Cara and back again before shrugging and turning around. Cara watched him stumble away wrinkling her nose at the foul odour that poured off him in waves.

"So I'm your girlfriend am I?" Cara giggled having finally found her breath. Jed's cheeks turned red. Instead of answering her, he held out a hand go help her up. She placed her palm in his feeling the same spark she'd felt when he'd touched her cheek in the forest.

"I thought you were in a hurry to get to my brother." He huffed, clearly embarrassed.

"I am. So take me to him." Cara ordered feeling a new sense of urgency now that they were on the inside. She had no desire to be inside the village longer than she needed to be.

They ran along the wall with Jed in the lead. Cara could see down into the village. She was amazed at the size of the village inside. There were rows and rows of wooden houses lined up around a huge square directly in the middle of the village. She could see over every single roof top. People were milling around a market in the village square. The hustle and bustle of the village hit her ears hard and loud. It was the source of the noise she'd heard so many times from the mountain only now it was so much louder.

She struggled not to scream against the ringing pain in her ears as she followed Jed down the stone steps onto the muddy streets. Pushing through crowds of people made her feel claustrophobic. She felt as though every person were staring at her. She found herself grinding her teeth, struggling to keep herself under control. *How many of these people have killed my family?* She asked herself as she tried to keep her head down, keeping Jed in her line of sight at all times.

It seemed like a lifetime had passed before they stopped although it had only really been a few minutes. They stood in front of one of the larger houses. It sat on a stone base. Cara could smell the scent of herbs coming from inside. Smoke came from the chimney. Jed charged up the steps and opened the door without even knocking. Cara followed him. She stopped on the threshold of the house. Inside the house was open plan. It had a large stone fireplace that was burning brightly. A wooden table and chairs stood at one end of the room while there were a few wooden benches at the other side. Cara felt sick as she saw a wolf pelt that was covering the floor like a rug in front of one of the benches.

"Come on." Jed shouted to her, "Close the door before someone sees you."

She stepped inside mentally shaking herself as she closed the door behind her. Jed was already heading up the stairs that lay behind the wooden table. His footsteps were hurried as he charged upward. Cara took a deep breath and headed up after him. On the landing there were three doors. The middle door was open. Cara could see Jed knelt down beside a wooden bed with a mattress made of straw. The window was covered by wooden shutters that blocked out the sunlight. The only light in the room was that of a small candle on the bedside table. As Cara watched Jed she noticed the boy lay on the bed. He was tossing and turning as he made a low groaning sound, clutching his forearm to his chest.

"It's ok Jasper," Jed whispered to his brother, "You'll be better soon."

"Please, get in here." Jed urgently gestured her inside. Cara held her breath as she walked over to his side. Seeing how much Jasper was wriggling she turned to Jed,

"You're going to have to hold him down while I take a look." She explained. Jed looked scared as he reached forward and pinned his brother to the bed. Jasper only wriggled more until Jed was lying over him, pinning him down with his own body. Cara moved around him and grabbed hold of Jasper's arm by the elbow. His skin was slick with sweat and his dark hair was plastered to his forehead. He looked completely feverish. Taking a deep breath, she held it in as she unwrapped the blood stained bandage from his wound. She gasped as she saw the wound. It was a huge bite. Blood and puss was oozing from the wound. His veins were turning black as the venom pulsed through his body.

"This is bad." She whispered to herself as she stared at the wound.

"What is it? What's happening to him?" Jed asked. Cara sighed and placed Jasper's wounded arm back on his chest.

"You can let go of him now." She told Jed. He removed himself from his brother, who calmed a little and turned to look at her.

"What is it?" he demanded again.

"The venom is definitely attacking his system." She explained after thinking of how to tell him.

"So is he going to die?"

"I'm not sure. All I can do is heal his wound. The rest is up to him." She explained. Without another word she knelt down beside the bed and raised her wrist to her mouth. Biting down on her wrist like she had in the forest, she drew blood and held it above Jasper's arm.

"Hold still." She told him as she placed her other hand on his shoulder to steady him. As though her touch had calmed him he became more still and she allowed her blood to drip onto his wound. Jasper let out a relieved sigh as though his wound had stopped hurting and he became completely still. Cara watched as his wound slowly began knit and heal together like Jed's had.

"Jed, what the hell is going on?" a deep voice suddenly demanded from the bedroom door. Cara turned to see a tall man with dark brown hair. He looked a lot like Jed but older and broader.

"What the hell is she doing?" The man bellowed. He stomped into the room and shoved Cara hard away from the bed. Cara saw his shoulders tense as he looked down at his brother's forearm. His wound had almost completely healed and the last slithers of skin were forming together.

"What kind of witchcraft is this?" The man demanded as he turned on Cara, "witches are not welcome in this house." Cara stood her ground even though the man struck fear into her very core. There was something beastly about him. He looked as though he could rip a wolf limb from limb.

"She's not a witch," Jed snapped at the man as he stepped between them, shielding Cara with his body, "be grateful. She just saved our brother's life." Cara wanted to remind him that that might not be quite true but she held her tongue as she saw how furious his older brother still looked.

"I will not be grateful to anyone who uses black magic." He almost sounded as though he was growling.

"Stop shouting." A small voice came from the bed. All three of them looked around to see that Jasper had sat up and was rubbing his temples. Jed raced forward and dropped down onto the bed, hugging his brother tightly.

"Jasper, you're ok." His voice was filled with glee but Cara felt a cold sense of dread spreading in her stomach. The venom was not killing him which meant only one other option. Even with the shutters over the window Cara could sense that night was fast approaching. She knew from the stories that the first night of the change was the worst. They were running out of time.

"I want you out of my house now." The huge brute that was Jed's brother snarled. He turned and grabbed Cara by the waist. Hoisting her over his shoulder he carried her out of the room and down the stairs. She kicked and screamed trying to get free but the grip of one arm was like iron. She felt as though he was crushing her rib cage with his mighty fingers.

Reaching the front door he swung it open and threw her down on the porch. She tumbled forward with a feeble scream as she toppled down the steps. She lay battered and bruised in the mud at the bottom.

"Leave and never come back or I'll rip your pretty little head off your dainty little shoulders." He grumbled. Cara remained still until he slammed the door shut. Then she sat up and pulled her lank muddy hair from her face.

"That's the thanks I get." She huffed as she picked herself up.

Looking around she was glad to see that the streets had emptied. The last light of the day was pouring down casting long shadows against the wooden huts. Cara walked around the side of the house and remained hidden in the shadows. As the light faded a woman appeared from the next street carrying a basket of bread and vegetables. She crossed the street, holding up her skirts and climbed the steps of the house. She was a middle aged woman. Her hair was covered by a cream hood but Cara could see the wrinkles on her hands as she reached to open the door. As she did Jed's older brother appeared again. The woman jumped nearly falling back down the steps. He grabbed her with a much gentler grip than he had Cara.

"Gilly you scared the living daylights out of me." The woman gasped, clutching her chest and trying to catch her breath.

"Sorry mam," Gilly apologised gently. Cara couldn't believe the giant's tender tone. It was as though he was a completely different person to the man who had thrown her down the stairs.

The woman looked at the sword that was strapped to her son's belt and sighed,

"You're not on hunting duty again are you?" She clutched her throat now as though she was trying to hold in a sob, "you know how I worry."

"Yes mam and you worry too much. I'll be fine. You should run up to Jasper. He's awake." Gilly explained. His mother looked shocked as he leaned forward and placed a kiss on her forehead before bouncing down the steps and disappearing down the street.

***

Jed sat a rocking chair beside Jasper's bed watching the shadows from the candle flicker on his brother's sleeping face. It was deadly silent in the room now that Jasper was finally sleeping peacefully. Jed kept looking at his brother's chest holding his breath until he saw the gentle rose and fall that signalled he was still alive.

The creaking of floorboards came from the stairs. The sound of rapid footsteps coming toward him made Jed jump out of his seat.

"What's happened? Is he ok? Gilly said Jasper was awake." Jed's mother's worried voice hit his ears as he turned to see her rushing toward the bed. Jed hushed her placing his index finger over his lips.

"He's resting now." Jed could see his mother's eyes moving over her son's forearm as if she was searching for the wound.

"How can it be?" She gasped as she gently ran her fingertips over the smooth tanned skin where the wound had been. Jasper stirred and turned over nodding back off instantly.

"How did this happen?" She asked as she turned to Jed. Her hazel eyes were filled with wonder as she stared at him waiting for an answer.

"A friend healed him," Jed explained, "Gilly threw her out before I got a chance to thank her. He called her a witch."

"Well any witch who saves the life of my son is welcome in this house." Jed was surprised to hear his mother speak in such a way. She was usually the one who denied the existence of anything supernatural.

"You must go and find her. I wish to thank her." His mother shooed him with a flicking gesture of her hands.

He turned and rushed down the stairs excited at the thought of seeing Baccara again. As he opened the front door and stepped out onto the porch he suddenly thought of something. He had no idea where she had gone.

Another Human

Cara felt as though she'd been hiding in the shadows for hours. She was leaning against the wooden wall when she heard a door creak open. She sprang up straight and peered around the side of the house. Relief filled her as she saw Jed stood on the porch. He looked confused as though thoughts were swimming through his head and he didn't know what to make of them.

"Jed!" Cara hissed at him. He jumped and glanced around quickly. Waving her hand at him, she gestured him over. He rushed to the end of the porch and jumped down beside her.

"Have you been out here the whole time?" he asked, "What happened to you?" his eyes were roaming up and down her body. She was covered in mud and she could feel the bruises swelling up all over her body.

"Well I couldn't leave. Your brother needs me," Cara huffed, "Your brother didn't really help though."

"I'm sorry about him." Jed removed a strand of her hair from her face and placed it behind her ear. She felt a tingle on her cheek as his hand brushed her skin.

"Mam wants you to come inside." He said suddenly making her stomach flip. Curiosity welled up inside her as she asked,

"Why?"

"She wants to thank you. We're not all monsters like my brother." He told her.

"I don't handle well facing humans." Cara replied feeling a little nauseous at the thought of meeting yet another human.

"Well I never would have guessed. You seem fine with me." Jed laughed. Before she could say another word he grabbed her wrist and began to pull her back toward the house.

"Jed what are you doing?" she screamed as she tried to pull her arm free. He smiled sheepishly at her as he continued to pull her toward the house.

The next thing she knew she was stood in the kitchen again. The wolf skin rug seemed to stare at her as she stood close to the front door. The woman she'd seen entering the house was now stood by the fire stirring something that hung in a pot over the flames. She had removed her hood and Cara could now see that she had dark brown hair that was tinted with silver and grey. As she turned to look at Cara she saw that her face was wrinkled disturbing a beauty that once was.

"Mam, this is Baccara." Jed pulled Cara around the table and the door slammed shut behind them.

"Baccara its lovely to meet you," Jed's mother moved forward and held out her hand to her, "Please call me Liz." Her hazel eyes sparked with suspicion as Cara stared down at her hand.

"Shake it." Jed whispered into Cara's ear. Cara raised her hand quickly and shook her hand. The suspicion disappeared from Liz's face.

"I believe I have you to thank for saving my son." Liz smiled as she moved forward. Cara felt herself tensing as Liz wrapped her arms around her, "How can I ever repay you?"

Cara felt relieved as Liz let her go and moved away. She shook her head and took a moment to think of what to say.

"There's no need to repay me."

"Now don't be silly." Liz brushed off with a flick of her wrist, "I remain the mother of three all thanks to you. There must be something I can do for you."

"Maybe she could stay for tea." Jed suggested. Cara shot him an angry look as Liz clapped with joy and replied,

"That's an excellent idea Jed."

"Oh no I couldn't. I have to get home to my family. My mother will be wondering where I am." Cara protested.

"Oh well I know how mothers worry. Maybe another time then?" Liz asked. Cara nodded almost too quickly.

"Is it already if I check on Jasper before I leave?" Cara asked. Liz smiled and rubbed Cara on the shoulder making her quiver inside.

"You're such a caring young girl," Liz smiled, "Go ahead."

Cara did her best to smile back before turning and heading up the stairs. Looking over her shoulder she saw that Jed was following her. She stopped at the top of the stairs and shoved his shoulder with her hand.

"What the hell was all that? Are you trying to kill me?" she hissed under her breath at him. Jed only giggled which made her turn and storm off into Jasper's room.

As soon as she entered the room she knew something was wrong. Jasper was nowhere to be seen. The bed covers had been scattered on the floor. The sour scent of fear filled the room. As she glanced around she heard the huffy sound of shallow breathing. A flicker of movement in the corner of the room made her look around. Crouched in the corner behind the rocking chair was Jasper. He was clutching at the arm of the chair and seemed as though he was rocking back and forth on his heels.

Cara took a deep breath and moved slowly toward him. Crouching down a little way off, she began to talk quietly to him,

"Jasper its ok. My name is Cara. I'm here to help you." Now that she was closer she could see the claw marks on the wooden floor. She could see the black tips to his fingers that were ripped and bleeding. The change had begun.

"What's happening to me?" Jasper asked as Jed appeared in the doorway. He was about to rush toward his brother when Cara raised a hand to gesture him to stop.

"Stay where you are." She told him before turning back to Jasper. He stared at her with eyes that were filled with fear of the unknown. He was shaking like a leaf. Cara leaned forward and placed a hand on his shoulder.

"It's alright kid. Everything is going to be fine." She promised. Turning back to Jed she asked,

"How do we get him out of the house without your mother seeing?" Jed looked shocked at her question and his mouth flapped a little before he answered,

"The window is probably the only way," He gestured toward the shuttered curtain, "But it's not safe out there at night." Cara glared at him and let a low growl escape from her throat.

"Ok fair point." Jed raised his hands in mock surrender.

"Jasper I need you to trust me ok?" Cara asked still holding his shoulder. She looked into his eyes waiting for him to respond. Finally he nodded. She removed her hand from his shoulder and held it out palm up. After a moment's hesitation he took her hand with his and allowed her to pull him to his feet.

"Good." Cara smiled at him as she heard a bolt being removed from the shutters. She turned to see Jed pulling the shutters open.

"Now we are going to go on an adventure." Cara told the young boy who clutched to her hand as though he was too afraid to let go. He still looked hesitant but he didn't protest as she led him over to the window.

"Do you trust me?" Cara asked as she looked down at him. Jasper stared up at her with eyes as round as the full moon. He looked tormented.

"Jasper I need you to trust me." Cara urged.

"You can trust her Jasper." Jed promised.

"I do." Jasper's voice shook.

"Ok then. I want you to follow me and do as I do." Cara explained to him. With some difficulty she removed her hand from his and climbed onto the bed. Sat on the edge of the windowsill she could see the muddy street below. It would be an uncomfortable landing but unlike a human she could make the drop without too much damage.

Taking a deep breath she pushed herself off the sill. She heard both boys gasp as she went over. Spinning in mid-air she bent her legs and landed on her feet. The shock of hitting the floor ran up all the way through her body. She held out her arms to steady herself and looked up to see Jasper and Jed peering over the sill at her.

"Jasper I need you to jump." Cara told them, "Jed meet us on top of the wall."

"It will be swarming with guards." Jed protested.

"Then hurry up and get down here." Cara snapped, "Come on Jasper. You can do it. Just jump." He had positioned himself on the windowsill. He now looked pale and scared in the moonlight.

"Come on. Jump." Cara urged.

"Can't I just use the front door?"

"No, your mum thinks you're still poorly. She won't let you out of the house." Cara knew that if the boy was anything like her that he'd hate the thought of his mother keeping him locked up.

It worked. He hesitated no longer. In a few seconds he was hurtling toward the ground. Cara dodged out of the way. Jasper landed on all fours with mud covering his hands and knees.

"Better than I thought you'd do." Cara admitted shrugging her shoulders. Jasper groaned as he straightened himself up.

"I'll be down in a minute." They heard Jed call from the window.

It seemed forever until Jed was stood beside them. Cara pulled Jasper into the shadow of the hut as she heard something moving. She was relieved when she saw Jed come around the side of the house. He smiled brightly as he glanced up to look at her.

"Sorry. Mum was asking all sorts of questions." He apologised as he walked past her and continued walking. Cara gestured to Jasper and then began to follow him.

"Where are we going?" Jasper asked.

"We're going into the forest." Cara replied. She turned as she heard Jasper's footsteps halt. Jed stopped just in front of her.

"I am never going into the forest ever again." Jasper protested, "It's too dangerous."

"Jasper I can assure you nothing is going to hurt you in that forest anymore." Cara promised as she placed her hands on his shoulders, trying to reassure him, "The truth is that right now you're safer in the forest than you are in the village." Jasper looked at Cara for a moment before turning to look at Jed.

"What's she talking about?" he asked his brother in a small, pitiful voice. Jed moved forward and patted his brother on the head.

"Cara is taking us somewhere safe," he explained, "She has something to show you but she can't until we're in the forest."

"But why can't she show me now?" Jasper moaned.

"It's too dangerous here." Cara told him as she glanced around her. The sound of a dog howling came from the nearest house.

"We need to go." Cara urged them. Jed nodded and turned back to Jasper.

"You want to be a man don't you?" he asked. Jasper seemed to gulp out of fear and then nodded.

They kept to the shadows away from the prying eyes of the guards who stood watch on the wall. Cara knew that if she had been alone she wouldn't have had a clue where she was going. Every house and every street looked the same. The scents of dirt and human were so thick it was impossible to find her way using her nose. In the darkness everything looked even more foreboding. The houses loomed over her as though they were going swallow her whole. Before long she began to feel nauseous with the terror that being around so many humans caused.

A huge sense of relief washed over her as she saw the stone staircase that led up to the top of the wall. Soon she would be free to run through the forest, back where she belonged. The joy of those thoughts had her charging up the steps before she had really thought about it. She was stopped short at the top as a guard stepped out in front of her. To her disappointment it was not the drunk man from their earlier encounter. This man was sober and mean looking. With a gasp of shock she realised that it was in fact Gilly. Jed's older brother stood much like the stone wall they were standing on, blocking her view of the forest beyond.

"What do you think you're doing?" He demanded as Cara heard footsteps behind her. Gilly's eyes lit with surprise as he recognised his brothers. His voice deepened as he demanded, "What the hell is going on here?"

Without a second thought Cara pounced up into the air and bounded over him.

"Get him out of here!" She called over to Jed. Gilly had turned on her and was stomping toward her as she landed on her feet a few metres away. Turning on her heels she began to run along the wall, dodging out of the way of his massive hands as he tried to grab hold of her. As she glanced over her shoulder she could just see Jed and Jasper disappearing over the edge of the wall.

After running on a few more moments to give them chance to get far enough down that he wouldn't catch them she turned to face Gilly. He skidded to a halt having cornered her against a curve in the wall. This time she leapt she aimed for his chest. The impact was enough to send him falling backward. As he toppled to the floor she leapt from his chest and hit the stone running. Her eyes were locked on the area where Jed's head had disappeared. Leaning over the wall she was relieved to see that they were more than half way down. Flipping herself over the edge of the wall she began to join them in their descent. A wind whipped up pinning her against the wall as she climbed down.

By the time she reached the bottom her hands were red raw with scrapes and cuts but were already healing. She shook them for a moment to regain blood flow and turned to see Jasper and Jed already running to the safety of the trees. With her wolf abilities it only took her a few seconds to catch them up. Jed looked shocked as he looked over his shoulder to see her jogging at his side. She gave him a cheeky smile before picking up her pace and taking the lead.

"Follow me." She ordered. She was happy to hear their clumsy footsteps following her as they hit the tree line. A sense of calm washed over her as she became surrounded by the familiar redwood trees that had always offered her comfort and protection. She skidded to a halt and listened to the wind whispering through the trees. It was a much better sound than the hustle and bustle of the village. It was calm and quiet and allowed her to think.

It was a few minutes before Jed and Jasper caught her up. They stopped and bent over, gasping for breath, clutching their shaking knees for support.

"How do you run so fast?" Jasper panted.

It's easy when you're a wolf." Jasper's head whipped up and he stared at her in dismay. She had begun to change slowly so not to scare him too much. First she allowed her teeth to grow and her fingernails to lengthen into huge black claws. Then she allowed her fur to grow and her eyes began to glow a brilliant blue in the moonlight that filtered down through the trees. After a few moments she stood before them as the huge black wolf that she was. The white stripe on her shoulder sparkled like star shine. Jasper's mouth gaped open as Jed stepped forward and placed a hand on his shoulder for support. Cara could see the young boy's hands shaking.

"You can touch her if you want to." Jed told his brother. Cara felt angry at this. She was not a pet that could be patted and cuddled. She could rip out his throat there and then if she'd wanted to. But she didn't. Instead she stood motionless as Jasper's shaky hand moved toward her head. He stroked her forehead before quickly pulling his hand back.

After letting him stare a little longer she returned to her human form more quickly than she'd transformed the first time. Jasper still gaped at her.

"You really are a witch." Jasper gasped. Cara let out a low growl which made him flinch backward.

"I am not a witch. I do not cast spells or summon demons. I am a lycan and pretty soon you shall be too." She explained feeling no more patience. The insult of being called a witch more than once in one day had worn her nerves thin.

"What's she talking about Jed?" Jasper asked looking up at his brother with a nervous expression on his face.

"Listen and she will tell you." Jed assured him as he wrapped his arm around his brother's shoulder. They both looked expectantly up at Cara. She felt as nervous as the boy. She had never told anybody what she was about to tell him.

"Do you remember anything from the night you were attacked?" She asked him. Jasper looked thoughtful. He began to shake as though the thoughts were painful.

"It's ok, little brother." Jed promised as he gripped his brother more tightly, "Nothing is going to harm you now."

"I remember being bitten and I remember Jed killing the wolf." He explained. He then looked down at his forearm as though it was the first time he had realised his wound was completely healed.

"I remember you pouring liquid on the bite. It stopped hurting straight away."

"That's because my blood has healing properties and soon yours will too. When the wolf bit you he sealed your fate. You would either die or you would become like him. He probably meant to finish you off but when your brother saved you he gave you a second chance," Cara explained, "the wolf's venom runs through your veins and as it has not killed you it means sometime in the next few days you will go through your first. I know this because you jumped out of your bedroom window and landed on your knees without a scratch where a human would have broken his legs." Jasper stared at her as though he couldn't quite take it all in.

Cara was about to continue when she heard something moving behind her. A twig snapped alerting her to something big. She whipped around ready to protect the humans when Ivy pushed her way through the bushes.

"Cara, I've been looking everywhere for you!" She screamed as she rushed forward and pulled Cara into an embrace, "I've been so worried. Thorn told us you'd been with a human." Cara felt herself tense at her friend's words. Ivy had clearly felt it too. She let go of Cara and stared at her. Then she looked over her shoulder as though she'd felt more eyes on her. Her green eyes grew huge as she saw Jed and Jasper stood behind. A deep growl grew in Ivy's throat and she bared her teeth at them.

"Ivy, stop acting like an animal." Cara hissed as she shoved her friend's shoulder. Ivy turned to glare at her looking shocked,

"So what Thorn says is true?" She demanded.

"Well that depends on what he's said."

"He's been telling the pack all day that you turned in front of a human and saved him from a bear attack. He told us you'd healed the human's wounds and that you'd gone to the village." Ivy explained. Cara felt angry not only with Thorn but with herself. How had she not noticed he'd been following her the whole time.

"What has Alder said about it all?"

"He has accused Thorn of lying and he's been banned from the cave," Ivy explained, "if you don't go to the pack and confess he will be killed by the humans before day break."

"Jed there's a river to east from here. There's a hollow tree where you can be safe from prying eyes. Take Jasper there. I will be back at dawn." Cara explained.

As she was about to follow Ivy into the forest she felt fingers clasp her wrist. Turning she was unprepared for what came next. Jed's lips were suddenly on hers, his hands placed on her cheeks. She felt heat pour from his lips to hers and spread through her body. When he released her she was more than a little disappointed.

"Thank you for helping my brother," he told her, "Be careful out there."

Cara stood on the ledge outside the cave. The wind whipped her hair across her face as she braced herself for whatever lay inside. The moon had reached its highest point and would soon be descending the sky again bringing with it the dawn of a new day.

Darkness enveloped her as she stepped inside. The sound of voices came from deep within the mountain and she knew she would find most of the pack inside. Ivy had already gone in ahead and as Cara entered the cavern she saw her friend rushing toward Alder who was perched on the ledge overlooking the rest of the back as they milled about in small groups enjoying their day's catch. Cara stood in the entrance. She watched as Ivy whispered quickly in Alder's ear. His eyes grew wide and he turned to glare at Cara. She forced herself not to turn and run as Alder gracefully sprang to his feet and called out loudly,

"Pack gather round. Boulder, Coal, bring my niece to me." He ordered to huge men. They stepped forward and took Cara arm in arm, leading her to the ledge, through the crowd that was forming. Murmurs erupted echoing off the walls of the cave,

"I told you it was true."

"She has to be punished."

"Someone needs to find Thorn."

Cara held her breath as she was forced forward to stand below her uncle. "Are the accusations true? Did you show your true form to a human?" Alder spat. He no longer seemed like the kind, playful uncle she had once knew. He was now a towering brick wall of a beast who glared down at her with anger flaring his nostrils. Cara took a deep breath and nodded,

"I did." She did not try to sugar coat her answer. She knew they would not listen to her. In showing a human her true form she had risked the safety of her whole pack.

"Do you know the punishment for breaking the pack's oldest and most important law?" Alder demanded. Cara saw a twinge of discomfort in her uncle's body as he stared down at her.

"Yes." Cara looked down at her feet no longer able to look her uncle in the eye.

"The punishment is death." Alder's words caused a scream from somewhere in the crowd. Cara looked up to see her mother's horrified face.

"Alder you cannot do this. She is your niece!" Eva screamed at him but he did not listen.

"Cara you have until dawn to say your farewells. When the sun rises you will join your father in the next world." Alder sentenced. Her mother began to scream and weep. Cara wanted nothing more than to embrace her mother and tell her everything would be ok but she couldn't. Coal and Boulder grabbed her arms against and began to lead her away into one of the back caves to ensure she could not escape during the night.

***

An Execution

Jed and Jasper reached the river just before dawn. The water was flowing past lazily as they stepped out onto its bank. The sky was just beginning to grow light. Jed glanced around in search of the hollow tree Cara had been talking about. He couldn't see it yet. Gesturing to Jasper he began to lead his brother down the river bank in search of the tree.

One moment everything was silent and then there was the sound of something huge charging toward them through the trees. Jed grabbed his dagger from his belt and held it in front of him ready to fend off whatever was about to attack them.

The wolf skidded to a halt in front of them. Even though it showed no signs of hostility toward them Jed knew that it was not Cara. The wolf was much smaller than Cara and its fur was a bright ginger even in the predawn light. The air was filled with tension as the wolf reared and then stood on two legs. A moment later Cara's pack mate Ivy was stood in front of them.

"What do you want?" Jed demanded, still holding his dagger pointed at her chest. There was a deep frown on her face as she stared at him.

"You can put that down. I'll be dead by night fall anyway if my pack find out what I just did." She told him. His face twisted with suspicion as he asked,

"What are you talking about?"

"Look stop asking questions. As much as I hate to say this I need your help." Ivy explained as she suddenly grabbed the dagger effortlessly from his hand and threw it onto the mud.

"Cara is in trouble."

"What kind of trouble?" Jed asked. His heart suddenly beat faster and he struggled not to start running to search for her as he thought of what might be happening to Cara.

"When she told our pack leader that she'd shown herself to you he sentenced her to death." Ivy explained. Jed felt his whole world swaying. He placed his hand on the nearest tree trunk in an attempt to steady himself.

"He can't do that. She's done nothing wrong." Jasper protested suddenly. Jed felt too weak to stop him from speaking.

"He can. He is our pack leader and it has been law since the dawn of time that any Lycan who shows their true form to a human will be put to death for the safety of the pack."

Ivy explained to them. Jed suddenly pushed himself upright feeling a fresh wave of strength.

"I won't let that happen," He promised, "But you have to take me to her."

Ivy didn't say another word. Instead she nodded and turned to leave through the trees.

"What about me?" Jasper protested as Jed was about to follow. Jed stopped and turned to his brother.

"You need to stay here." He told him. Jasper instantly looked disappointed.

"But I'm the reason she's in this mess aren't I?" he protested, "I should be the one to fix it."

"The boy is right." Ivy had returned to the bank in time to hear what Jasper had to say, "He should come with us. Maybe if the pack see why she did what she did they might be more lenient." Jed quickly shook his head.

"I got you out of the village to get you out of trouble. I'm not going to let you come and get yourself into danger otherwise it was all for nothing." He told his brother.

"If you don't let me come when I turn into a wolf your head will be the first I bite off!" Jasper yelled as he puffed out his chest and raised his shoulders trying to look bigger. Jed turned an angry glare on Ivy as he heard her giggling behind him.

"I like him," she laughed as she pointed at Jasper, "You really need to let him come." she gestured for Jasper to follow her brother Jed even had a chance to reply.

"Well hey nobody ever listens to me anyway." Jed huffed throwing his arms up in the air. He grabbed his dagger from the mud where Ivy had thrown it before following them.

Cara tossed and turned all night. The stone floor of the cave seemed even more uncomfortable than usual. Images of the time she'd spent with Jed ran through her head like a blurred maze. His face seemed to haunt her as she imagined never seeing it again. As she thought about it she realised she would not have done anything differently even though her actions meant that in a few hours she would face her end. In a strange way she wasn't scared. It calmed her knowing that she would soon be with her father again.

She sensed the coming of dawn even before Coal and Boulder appeared from the entrance of the cave.

"It's time to go." Boulder's voice was gruff. Cara didn't protest. She stood and allowed herself to be led out of the cave. Holding her head high and taking a deep breath she stepped out into the main cavern. The rest of the pack were waking all around. Some were already murmuring among themselves. As she appeared they glanced up at her. Some had angry expressions while others looked sympathetic. Alder was stood beside the cave entrance waiting for them. Coal and Boulder pushed Cara roughly forward and forced her to walk toward him. Alder frowned as she stopped in front of him.

"It's time." He told her. Cara nodded unable to speak. She clasped her hands in front of her and followed him out of the cave. The fresh morning breeze flushed her cheeks as she stepped out onto the ledge. She breathed deeply feeling the air on her face, taking in the scents of the forest. The sun was just beginning to rise above the horizon. Alder jumped down off the ledge and began to head down the mountainside toward the thicker trees. Cara followed suite with Coal and Boulder on either side of her. They matched her stride for stride. Even if she'd wanted to run they would have caught her within a few seconds. She was no match for two grown male wolves and she knew it. With that said she accepted her punishment. She had known the law when she'd made the decision to help Jed. She accepted that she had to pay the price.

The sounds of many feet moving through the forest came from behind Cara and she knew that many of the pack had followed them. She had no idea whether her mother would be among them but she prayed that she wasn't. She couldn't handle the thought of her mother seeing her execution.

They stopped in a large glade where the first flowers of spring had begun to blossom. Birds had begun to sing their first morning song. It scared Cara to think how easily the world continued to revolve even as she faced death. Alder walked into the middle of the clearing and turned to face Cara. She moved forward and stood a few paces opposite him. Coal and Boulder remained at her side the whole time.

The rest of the pack began to file into the glade and circle around until they enveloped them. Cara stared at her uncle feeling brave as she looked at the man who's actions would soon be her death. The birds seemed to go quiet as he began to speak,

"This morning we are here to pass justice for the crime of revealing our secret to a human," he called loudly enough for the whole pack to hear. Some cheered while others murmured small protests that would not make any difference to her fate, "For this treachery the sentence is death. Cara Ironblood, blood of my blood, do you have anything to say before a pass the sentence?" Cara continued to look into her uncle's eyes noticing out indifferent he seemed to the whole situation. For a stranger looking on the scene nobody would have guessed that she was his niece.

"All I have to say is that if I could go back and do it all again I would. I believe I did the right thing and that my father would have been proud of me." A loud shockwave of gasping erupted all around her.

"Alder please don't do this!" came her mother's voice. Cara glanced to her left to see two pack members holding her mother at the front of the crowd.

"It is the law." Alder replied to his sister-in-law, "I must do what is right for my pack."

"You don't have to do this. You don't have to prove anything to anyone." Eva protested. Alder shook his head and growled at her,

"I am the leader of this pack. I have passed judgement and I will carry out this sentence." He glared at Eva for a few seconds before turning back to Cara.

"Do you have anything else to add?" he asked. Cara shook her head.

Alder seemed to take a sharp intake of breath before stepping forward and placing a hand on each side of her head. Boulder and Coal gripped her arms holding her in place. Cara felt her uncle's grip tightening on her head as he readied to break her neck.

"Stop!" there was a loud scream from the edge of the glade. Alder kept his hands on her head but turned to look in the direction of the voice. Cara could just see out of the corner of her eye that the crowd was parting to let someone through. Cara was shocked to see Jed appear through the pack. Behind him came Jasper and to Cara's surprise Ivy. The pack began to shrink away and growl as if they were frightened of Jed.

"Ivy, what is the meaning of this?" Alder demanded as he removed his hands from Cara's head.

"I can't let you do this." Ivy explained.

"We can't let you do this." Jed corrected her. He glanced as Ivy as he stepped forward. Cara wanted to run to him and tell him to get away but she couldn't. Coal and Boulder still held her in an iron tight grip.

"You have no right to be here boy," Alder growled, "I could rip your throat out just for interrupting."

"You could but then you wouldn't get to hear what I have to say." Jed's words were confident but Cara could see the fear glinting in his eyes. It was clear he knew he was in danger. She saw his eyes flicker from side to side at the pack who had now remade the circle.

"Why would I have any interest in what you have to say?" Alder demanded.

"If you had no interest you would have killed me already." Jed's brave words made Cara tense with fear.

"Speak quickly or never speak again." Alder growled, removing his hands from Cara's head and turning to face Jed with a scowl on his face.

"What if I found a way to end the war between man and wolf?" Jed asked. Murmurs rose up around the glade and even Cara found herself gaping at him. Alder raised his hand for silence and gestured for Jed to continue.

"Maybe if the villagers realise that one of their own is a wolf they might be less willing to kill your kind." Jed suggested as he pointed toward his brother.

"Eva, examine him." Alder ordered. Cara watched her mother wipe tears from her eyes before moving over to Jasper who stood bravely beside Ivy. She roughly began to examine his face, holding his chin and turning his head from side to side. Then she grabbed his arms and pulled up each sleeve. When she came to the arm which had been bitten she froze. Cara knew she'd seen the black veins that were spreading up his arm. She turned to Alder and told him,

"He's definitely been bitten." She then turned to look at Cara with a suspicious scowl on her face, "If you did this not even the boy can save you." Cara was about to speak when Ivy stepped forward,

"It wasn't Cara. It was the intruder who we found dead close to the village. I remember smelling the boy's scent at the scene." she explained, looking Alder in the eye as though she was mentally willing him to believe her.

"Then how do you propose getting the villagers to listen to you? As soon as they see him turn they will turn on him and kill him." Alder explained, pointing his finger at Jasper while speaking as though he wasn't even there.

"Let me worry about that," Jed told Alder, "All I'm asking for is that if I can end this war you will give Cara her life." Alder seemed to be turning the idea over in his mind for a few moments.

"You have two days," Alder finally told Jed. He then turned to Coal and Boulder, "Take her back to the cave. Don't let her out of your sight." The two men nodded and began to jostle Cara back the way they had come.

***

Unlikely Alliances

Jed was about to leave the glade when he heard footsteps approaching him. He turned to see a tall broad shouldered man behind him. He looked as though he was only a little older than Jed with short black hair. His eyes were a smoky grey that glinted in the early morning light. His expression was unreadable as he stood and looked down at Jed.

"I'm coming with you." The man's words shocked Jed to the core. He stared at him for a few moments wondering what to say.

"Why would you want to come with us?" he finally asked. The man looked down at his hands and fiddled his thumbs around a little before looking back at Jed.

"Well I'm guessing you heard that Lord Edgar's son went missing four years ago?" he asked. Jed nodded wondering where the conversation was going.

"Well that son was me," the man looked as though he was ashamed and couldn't look Jed in the eye, "I was bitten on my first hunt. Alder found me during my change and brought me to the pack and I've been here ever since but I've been thinking of returning to see my father every day since."

"So you're telling me that you're Edward?" Jed stared at the man open mouthed.

He remembered his father returning from a hunt with the news that Lord Edgar's son had been lost. The whole village had assumed he'd died in the cold of the forest. They had never imagined that such a young boy could have survived in the wilderness.

"I go by Fang here." The man shrugged. "Do you really think your father will expect you back when he knows what you are?" Jed heard Ivy's voice behind him. He turned to see her walking toward them. Having been so interested in his conversation with Fang he hadn't noticed her lurking in the bushes. She stopped beside him, never once taking her eyes off Fang.

"To those people we are nothing but mindless animals. They would waste no time in jamming a knife between your ribs if they knew the truth about you." She growled as she pointed in the direction of the village.

"That may be true but aren't you tired of the constant fear of being hunted down?" Fang protested, "Cara clearly saw something in them to save one of them and from what I remember not every villager was a killer. There were women and children too. Women who just wanted their families to be safe."

"Fang is right. If we could find a way to convince the villagers that peace between men and wolves will ensure the safety of their families then we can end this war and the killing will end." Jed told Ivy. He then turned and looked in the direction where the two brutish men had forced Cara off into the bushes, "beside s I have to try or what chance does Cara have?" Ivy sighed and looked down at her feet for a moment as though she was thinking. When she looked up again Jed saw a flame of energy inside he deep green eyes that he'd not seen before.

"Then I guess you're going to need some help," she suddenly smiled a smile that held a thousand meanings, "I'm coming with you."

The journey back down the mountain took them until the sun had reached its highest point and begun to go down again. Weak rays of sunlight lit the forest floor as they drew close to the edge of the trees. Jed was breathing heavily with the effort of keeping up with Ivy and Fang. Their legs carried them quicker than any human could possibly walk and yet something told Jed they were holding back so that he could keep up. Even Jasper seemed hardened against the effects of the fast pace. Jed found himself shaking off the thought as he realised it probably had something to do with the wolf venom coursing through his brother's blackening veins.

They reached the shingle road that led to the gates of the village just before dusk. As they trudged along the sounds of the villagers readying for the night ahead grew louder. He could feel the eyes of many guards peering down on him from the top of the wall as they neared the gates.

"Halt!" A deep, angry voice shouted as a multitude of spearheads were jabbed down close to their faces, barring their way. At least six guards stood before them holding their weapons out to create a barricade.

"State your names and business." The guard directly in front of them ordered. Jed was about to speak when Fang stepped forward.

"My name is Edward Stronghammer. I wish an audience with my father Lord Edgar Stronghammer." Jed was shocked by Fang's strong, commanding voice. He stood bravely with his shoulders and chin held high. The guards all glanced at each other looking confused.

"Lord Edgar's son is dead. State your name and business." The guard who had spoken before spoke again.

"I have stated my name and my business now take me to my father." Fang demanded in a cool, calm voice as though he was used to giving orders.

"I will take them in." A voice sounded behind the guards. Jed had to stand on tip toes to see the man who had spoken. Instantly Jed knew who he was from the bright purple tunic he wore with the emblazoned bear rearing proudly on his chest. He was Frederick Stonehammer, Lord Edgar's younger brother and Fang's uncle.

"Let them through." He ordered with a flick of his leather gloved hand as the guards turned looking dumbstruck, "if it is an audience with Lord Edgar they want it is an audience they shall get." The guards suddenly jumped into action forming a circle around Jed and the others. They began to shove them forward. Frederick took the lead, heading through the village toward the main square.

Jed was struck with admiration as he always was when he stepped into the main square. It was the most beautiful place in the whole village. Compared to the dark muddy back streets where his house was situated it was a large open space paved with white brick that surrounded huge fountain that featured a huge white stone bear much like the one on Frederick's tunic. Across the square were the huge marble steps that led to Lord Edgar's manor. The huge building towered above the rest with towers to the east and west. Beautiful climbing roses in all shades of red, yellow and pink covered the front of the building. It was a magnificent sight that took Jed's breath away every time he saw it. Never in his wildest dreams had he ever thought he might actually see the inside of the most beautiful building he'd ever seen in his life.

Now as he approached the steps of the building he felt weak at the knees. He dreaded the thought of what might happen on the other side of the huge iron doors once they entered. He felt Ivy walking tensely beside him and remembered how Cara had acted while in the village. He felt sorry for her as she flinched at every jerking movement of the guards all around her.

When they reached the top of the steps the iron doors swung open to reveal a lobby that was filled with stuffed wolves and fur rugs. Paintings of the lords and ladies who had lived in the house were dotted all over the walls. Jed reached out and grabbed hold of Ivy's hand as she let out a horrified gasp at the sight in front of her. Glancing at her he saw the tears springing to her eyes and squeezed her hand hoping to comfort her even a little.

They continued forward without halting through a huge stone archway and down a long corridor where yet more fur rugs lay. Jed saw how both Fang and Ivy did their best not to stand on the rugs within the restrictions the guards had placed on them.

When they finally stopped it was because a smaller door blocked their path.

"Wait here." Frederick ordered before slipping through it. The guards remained in formation around their charges until he returned.

"That will be all, thank you." Frederick told the men with a flock of his hand to signal that they were dismissed. He then turned to Jed and the others and added, "Lord Edgar has agreed to see you, follow me." As the guards dispersed Jed followed Frederick through the door followed by the others.

He was even more amazed at the sight that met his eyes know. He had entered what looked to be a huge throne room that might be situated inside a king's castle. The walls towered topped by a ceiling that was painted with many different shades of colour depicting image after image of battles fought between man and wolf. Huge stone columns circled the room holding up a balcony that overlooked a stage where a huge stone throne stood. Perched on the throne was Lord Edgar. He looked magnificent dressed in all his finery. He looked much different from the last time Jed had seen him in his drab brown hunting gear. He wore a royal blue tunic and crisp clean cream trousers the liked of which Jed had never seen. Sat beside him in a smaller but no less beautiful chair was his wife Margret. She wore a long flowing dress of mint green silk that contrasted well against her beautiful blonde hair which cascaded over her left shoulder. Though she looked young and beautiful Jed could see the tell-tale signs of age in the wisdom that shone from her green eyes as she gazed upon them.

"Come forward." Edgar ordered gesturing them to approach him. Jed moved forward with Jasper at his side. He could feel Ivy and Fang moving much more curiously behind him. Jed and Jasper dropped to their knees as though they were in the presence of a king and from the look of satisfaction on Edgar's face Jed could tell that the others had done the same.

"Please rise." The lord ordered. Jed stood still keeping his eyes turned toward the ground. He remembered his father teaching him about how to stand when in the presence of the privileged and did his best to follow his instructions now.

"Aren't you Stoneshield's sons?" Edgar asked sounding intrigued, "which one of you dares to say you are my son?" His voice had turned angry and Jed thought he heard a hint of pain as he listened to Edgar's words.

"Neither my lord." Fang spoke before Jed had a chance, "for I am your son." Fang stepped forward until he stood in front of his father. Jed hadn't noticed when but Fang had lifted his hood to cover his face which seemed to anger Edgar now as he looked down on him.

"Don't you know it's rude to hide your face in the presence of a lord?" Edgar demanded.

"Please allow me to apologise father." Fang replied as he dropped down onto his knees as though he was about to kiss Edgar's boot. The lord seemed as though he was about to protest when his mouth dropped open and a strangled gasp escaped him. Fang had lowered his hood and he lofted his face to look at Edgar.

"Edward!" Margret screamed suddenly. She flew from her chair, almost tripping on her dress, and threw herself down on the floor beside her son. Wrapping her arms around him she began to cover his face in kisses. Edgar sat looking shocked as he watched the scene in front of him. Jed watched his expression turn from one of denial to one of wonder.

"How is this possible?" Edgar demanded, "How has my son been returned to us?" He looked at Frederick who had remained close to the door. The lord's younger brother shrugged.

"You have Jed to thank for my return. He gave me the strength to face my fears." Fang explained as Margret finally came up for air. She did not release him though and her arms looked as though they were crushing him. Edgar turned to look at Jed,

"How can I ever repay you boy? Name anything and it will be done."

Jed could think of many things that he could have asked for right there and then but there was one thing at the top of his list. An image of Cara's smiling face lit at the back of his eyelids as he closed his eyes and took a deep breath before replying,

"We all wish for one thing." He told him. Lord Edgar looked intently at Jed as though waiting for him to continue.

"We wish for you to ban the killing of the wolves." Jed explained. The smile that had lit Edgar's face only moments before suddenly turned upside down. He scowled at Jed before glancing around the others in the room.

"What is the meaning of your request Jedidiah Stoneshield? What could possibly make you request such a thing?" He demanded. His voice was filled with anger at the request.

"He requests it because I am one of the wolves." Fang spoke up then removing himself from his mother's grip. She remained knelt in front of him with a confused look on her face that mirrored the one on Edgar's.

"What are you talking about boy?" Edgar demanded.

"The night I disappeared I clearly wasn't killed by a wolf but I was attacked by one," Fang explained, "the wolf bit me and left me for dead but I woke up the next morning feeling strange." Jed found himself searching Edgar's face for any kind of reaction as Fang continued, "The wolf's bite had poisoned me. I could feel the venom in my veins and I knew it was spreading. At first I didn't know what was happening but when I realised I knew I couldn't come home. I had been turned and I was a danger to the whole village."

"Have you gone mad?" Edgar demanded. Fang shook his head.

"I can prove it." He replied. Edgar looked as though he was about to speak again when Fang took a step backward.

Jed watched as Fang's body began to change. First his fingers began to lengthen into sharp pointed black claws. Then his nose began to elongate and darken. Before long there was a huge black wolf stood in the middle of the throne room. Margret screamed scrambling away from her son. Edgar had risen to his feet and was gaping at his son who stood with his head bowed and his shoulders lowered as though he was surrendering. Jed heard the scrape of metal on metal and turned to see that Frederick had removed his long sword from it's sheathe on his belt. He looked as though he was about to attack Fang when Edgar suddenly raised a hand to stop him, never once taking his eyed from his son. Jed found himself sucking in breath having not realised he'd been holding his breath.

"So the stories my father told me as a boy were true. Lycans really do live in the forest." Edgar's words shocked Jed. The only time he'd heard the word lycan was when Cara had first said it. He had not expected to hear it come from his leader's mouth. Fang returned to two legs and nodded.

"Now you see why you must stop the killing. You are not just killing mindless creatures you are slaughtering a species so close to your own that it is murder." He explained to his father.

"I must have time to consider this and speak with my council." Lord Edgar spoke suddenly. He then gestured Frederick forward. His brother moved forward and knelt his knee in a bow, waiting for his brother to give him his orders.

"You will see that these people are taken to the guest quarters and properly cared for." Edgar explained. Frederick nodded before straightening up and turning to Jed and the others.

"Please follow me." He told them. Jed fell into line behind Fang as he followed Frederick back through the door they entered through. Outside two guards were now stood on either side of the door. They stood to attention as Frederick exited the throne room.

"We are to take our guests to the guest quarters." He explained to the two guards who instantly nodded and began to lead the way down the corridor.

They walked back through the house and rounded the staircase, heading upstairs toward the bedchambers. The guards led them down another corridor to the left. Jed found himself gazing at the many paintings of previous lords and ladies who had lived in the house. He couldn't believe how many there were. The paintings seemed to be endless. Having passed door after door they stopped at the end of the corridor where a large wooden door stood. One of the guards pushed the door open and stepped inside. He stepped to the side to allow the others to enter the room. It was a huge sitting room of well cushioned furniture. Flower vases held blooming bouquets of beautiful lilies and roses. There were five other doors leading off into other rooms and Jed guessed that they must be the guest bedroom.

"I shall place guards on the door. If you need anything please don't hesitate to ask them." Frederick explained, "I shall also send some service women for warm water so that you can all bathe." He looked each of them up and down as though he thought they were filthy. Without another word he turned and headed back out of the room. The two guards dipped their heads in respect before turning and following Frederick.

The Change

The hours passed by painfully slowly. By the time night fell Fang and Ivy had each retired to the bedrooms. Jed paced up and down the room sometimes gazing out the windows and other times staring at nothing.

Jasper who had collapsed into an exhausted state on one of the plump cushions sofas suddenly began to make a whimpering noise. Jed looked over to see that he had curled in on himself and was rocking back and forth like he had been when Cara had found him in the corner of his bedroom.

"What's wrong?" Jed demanded as he rushed to his brother's side dropping down onto his knees.

"My muscles hurt." Jasper's words were broken by gasps of pain as he clutched his arms across his chest as though he was trying to form a barrier against the pain. Jed placed a hand on Jasper's shoulder trying to comfort him. He was shocked by the heat radiating from his brother's skin underneath the material of his jacket.

"You're boiling. Let's get this coat off shall we?" Jed suggested.

"Jed don't touch him. Get up and back away slowly." Fang ordered as Ivy rushed in from behind him. She'd changed out of her dirty cotton shirt and brown leather trousers and was now wearing a silky white slip nightgown that flowed to the floor.

She raced to Jasper's side shoving Jed out of the way. "Move back unless you want to lose an arm." She growled at him as she blocked his view of his brother. Jasper's whimpering was slowly turning into gasping yelps of pain. Jed tried to reach for his brother again desperate to comfort him but Fang had sped around the sofa and grabbed hold of him. Jed fought with everything he had but he was no match for a grown adult Lycan and Fang pulled him aside easily.

"Jed calm down! Listen to me! You're in danger!" Fang yelled effortlessly managing to keep hold of Jed, "you can't help him while you're in this state." Suddenly registering Fang's words he began to calm, his body went limp in Fang's arms and he slowly released him.

"What's happening to him?" Jed ask turning to Fang. He tried to block out the screams of his brother but it was no use.

"He's changing for the first time which means until he gets meat you are in danger of losing your life. He won't turn on his own kind which means the only option left is you." Fang explained in a rushed tone.

"Fang I need help over here!" Ivy's voice was raspy and she sounded out of breath as though she'd run a marathon.

Hearing her voice set Fang into motion. He brushed past Jed and headed for the sofa. Jed turned to see Ivy using her whole body to pin Jasper down. His fingers had shortened and blackened much like Fang's had in the throne room and were beginning to look more and more like claws by the second. The sofa cushioning of the sofa had no protection as he dug his claws into the material ripping it with incredible ease. Jed felt a lump in his throat that he struggled to swallow as he saw Jasper's mouth gape open to reveal sharp pointed fangs. His whole body was shaking now and he fought hard against the weight of Ivy. Fang stepped forward and reinforced her grip, placing his hands on Jasper's shoulders and pushing him down into the cushioning.

"Jed this is around the time you should be running to that door and ordering the guards to fetch you as much fresh meat as possible unless you want your brother to carry the guilt of eating you for the rest of his life." As Ivy spoke Jed imagined feeling his brother's furred jaws clamping down on his throat and draining the life out of him. It sent his whole body shaking and as he reached the door he struggled to turn the handle with shaking hands. Just as he was about to push the door open there was a loud knocking of knuckles and the door swung open.

"What's going on in here? Is everybody alright?" The guard on the other side demanded. Jed was relieved that the guard was shorter than him and he managed to hide his brother from view no matter how much the guard tried to look around him.

"Everything is fine sir. My brother is just hungry. I wondered if perhaps you might be able to fetch us some meat?" Jed spoke as calmly as possible given the situation. The guard began to look suspicious as Ivy called over,

"Make sure it's fresh and raw."

"Please, it would be much appreciated." Jed added. As the guard nodded Jed quickly slammed the door on him.

"Jed, look out!" The warning came too late. Jed was suddenly thrown hard against the door. Hard rasping breath beat against his left ear as Jasper pinned him to the door. Terror filled Jed as he felt claws piercing his shoulder ripping through his fur jacket with ease. He tried to push back against his brother, desperate to get away but only helped the claws embed deeper. It was agony and even worse that his brother was causing it.

"Jasper stop! It's me. It's Jed. Come on kid it's me, your brother." Jed begged but to no avail. It only seemed to anger Jasper more.

"Don't let him bite you." Ivy screamed as Jed felt more than saw his brother's jaws moving toward the back of his neck. Jed did the only thing he could think of. He slammed his head backward into his brother's elongating face. The impact sent his head spinning but he felt the weight of his brother lifted as he gasped in shock and spiralled backward. As Jed turned to look into the burning eyes of his brother Fang grabbed hold of Jasper's arms pulling them behind his back. Jasper let out a blood curdling screech that brought tears to Jed's eyes.

Jasper fought with all his might against Fang as Ivy stepped between him and Jed. She placed her hands squarely on his chest and looked into his eyes as though she was trying to connect with him.

"Jasper I know you're in there and I know you're hurting but you need to listen to me," she spoke in a cool calm voice, "If you do this you can never go back from it. You will kill your brother and you will hate yourself forever." The words seemed to go straight over Jasper's head as he growled in her face. As though she was deeply offended her hand whipped out slapping hard across the face. Jed flinched at the sound of skin slapping skin. Jasper went silent for a few moments only to begin growling again.

Jed jumped at the sudden sound of knuckles rapping on the door behind him. The wood shook against his back. Turning quickly he opened the door just enough to see the same guard stood on the other side. In his hands he held a large wooden basket that was covered by a linen cloth.

"Thank you." Jed smiled as warmly as possible at the guard as he took the basket from him. The guard looked flustered as Jed closed the door on him yet again. As Jed closed the door Jasper began to make a low rumbling sound. His nose was moving from side to side as he sniffed the air. Jed guessed that he'd smelled the meat in the basket. He removed the cloth to reveal a heap of fresh blood red meat. The irony scent hit his nostrils instantly and he could only imagine what his brother was smelling.

"Pass it here." Ivy ordered raising her hands to take the basket. Jed passed it to her and she removed a large slab of meat placing the basket on the floor. She raised it up to Jasper's face allowing him to see and smell the meat before Fang slowly released him looking as though he was ready to pounce again if he needed to.

To Jed's relief Jasper was no longer interested in him. Instead he grabbed hold of the meat from Ivy's hands and began to cram it into his mouth, tearing at it easily with his sharp fangs. It took him less than a minute to finish the whole slab of meat that could have fed an entire family. Ivy removed another slab from the basket and held it up. Jasper seemed just as ravenous as before as he snatched the meat from her and continued eating. Jed watched in horror as he realised that that slab of meat would have been his throat if Ivy and Fang had not been there to restrain his brother. He found his hands rising to his neck, clutching his throat as though he was trying to protect it from his brother's view. Seeing him doing to Fang frowned and blocked Jed's view of his brother,

"You can relax now. He will calm down in a minute."

It took Jasper only five minutes to finish off the basket. Jed was relieved to see that he had calmed by the time it was finished. He crouched on the ground with blood-stained hands. The crimson liquid also covered his face almost right the way to his eyes. His eyes had softened and his fingers were beginning to return to normal when Jed asked Ivy,

"Why hasn't he turned completely?" Ivy giggled as she watched Jasper looking at his hands in wonder.

"Don't be silly. The change doesn't happen overnight. It will be about a week before his full change and another few before he can master changing at will." she explained as Fang moved over to Jasper and began to whisper in his ear.

"Will he be ok?" Jed asked. He couldn't help but feel worried for his brother. After seeing how much pain he'd gone through he was getting more worried by the hour that it might be too much for him.

"He'll be fine once he's settled into a pack and has others around him that he can relate to." Ivy answered.

"A pack? Won't he come home with you?" Ivy shrugged and continued to look at Jasper as his eyes widened at whatever Fang was telling him.

"If the pack accepts him then that's great if not he will have to learn to survive on his own until he can join another pack or start one of his own." Jed gulped down his fear as he heard her words.

"What are the chances of the pack accepting him?"

"If all goes well with our plans and he helps to stop this war then the chances are good. If not he has pretty much no chance."

Sudden hammering on the door made him jump. He whipped his head round to see the door fling open. Frederick stepped inside followed by a huge number of guards. Taken by surprise Jed jumped to his feet and glanced around the room as the guards filed in. he felt an iron grip on his elbow and looked around to see that one of the guard's had hold of him.

"What is the meaning of this?" Fang demanded as two guards grabbed each of his arms and pulled him away from Jasper.

"The council has decided that you will all stand before the whole village to plead your case." Frederick explained. He then gestured to the guards and they began to roughly move the whole group out of the room.

"Don't I at least get to dress?" Ivy hissed angrily at the guards. They seemed to ignore her as they led her away.

Jed was forced into line as Frederick took the lead. He stumbled nearly tripping over the guard in front and received a clip over the head for his trouble. The sharp pain only lasted a few seconds but a throb remained. Glancing over the shoulder of the guards behind him he saw that Jasper was behind. There seemed to be more guards around him than the rest of them as though they were suspicious of the blood that dripped from his face onto his white shirt.

The group was led back down the corridor, down the stairs and through the front door. Jed blinked his eyes against the dawn light that hit him as he exited the house. He was amazed to see that already huge groups of people had begun to enter the village square. News spread quickly in such a small village but he hadn't thought there would be so many people already. He glanced around the square looking for the familiar faces of his parents and older brother. He was disappointed when he didn't see them. The guards shoved them down a few steps and then stopped.

"Don't move," Frederick ordered, "There are archers ready to shoot if you try anything stupid." He gestured to the roof of the building. Jed looked up to see that indeed there were at least ten men with bows aimed right at them. The lump in his throat returned as he imagined an arrow head piercing his heart. It made him quake with fear.

The square was steadily filling up. The people at the front of the crowd who could see the group most clearly were shouting threats and taunts as though they had already decided that they were guilty of some awful crime. Jed felt his hope dwindling as he looked at the angry faces of the people he had called friends and neighbours.

The doors that had closed behind them creaked. Jed looked up to see Lord Edgar and his wife escorted by a huge group of guards. Lord Edgar remained in the clothes he'd been in the last time Jed had seen him and he realised that the council must have been talking all night. His face twisted with regret as he glanced at his son who was still in the grip of the guards.

He turned toward the crowd of people who had quietened at his appearance and raised his hand in greeting to them all. Then he glanced at the group of prisoners again before addressing the whole crowd,

"Good people of Piearre we stand here today to judge the fate of not just these four people but also the life of a whole species." He explained. A murmuring sound began to grow louder among the crowd as they glanced at one and other. Jed could hear some of the things they were murmuring to each other as the murmurs grew into shouts,

"What is he talking about?"

"What have they done?"

"We want answers!"

"Silence!" Lord Edgar ordered as he raised one hand into the air to gesture everyone to be quiet. He used his other hand to take hold of Margret's. She looked as though she had been crying for hours. Her eyes were red and so puffy that she looked as though she could barely see. She clutched her husband's hand so tightly that Edgar almost looked as though he was in pain.

Once the crowd had quieted down Lord Edgar began to explain,

"Yesterday these four people entered my home. Many of you may have heard that one of them was my son," murmurs rose yet again only to be silenced by another raised hand, "it is true that my son Edward is among these prisoners." The eyes of the crowd turned from Edgar to the crowd as they searched for his son's face. Fang remained motionless as the eyes fell on him. He kept his gaze above their heads trying to look as though he didn't care.

"Although yes he is my son he is not the child that left this village. He has a dark secret that we are here to judge today." Edgar explained, "I have spoken with my council and have determined that the things these people ask for may be out of the reach of this village."

"That's not true!" Jed couldn't stop himself from shouting, "We are only asking for peace!"

"Peace is a hard thing to give if it means risking the lives of the people you are meant to protect!" Edgar snapped turning his angry gaze on Jed. Even though he wanted to look away Jed forced himself not to.

"If you are so determined to speak then you may explain what you are doing here." Margret spoke suddenly. Her voice was sharp and angry; much different from the soft welcoming voice of the mother who had welcomed her son home the day before. Edgar shocked Jed by nodding. He had expected him to object to his wife's demand but instead he agreed.

"Step forward and plead your case." He ordered gesturing for the guards to release him.

Jed took a deep breath and removed himself from the circle of guards. He moved up a few steps remaining one down from the Lord and Lady. Then he turned to look at the crowd. Every pair of eyes were attached to him. He closed his eyes for a few seconds and took a few deep breaths before opening them again and beginning, "A few days ago I met a girl in the woods. She'd been caught in one of our wolf traps." There were gasps of shock and horror as he explained how he'd cut her down and how she'd run off before he'd managed to find out who she was, "When I went into the forest again I found her again. This time we started talking but before I could get much information out of her we were attacked by a huge grizzly bear." Jed found himself beginning to enjoy his story telling as the crowd became more and more animated with every sentence.

"I would have died if it wasn't for the girl. She saved my life but she was much more complicated than I'd first thought. I'm sure you've all heard the stories that grandparents often tell their grandchildren to stop them from wandering into the woods but also sure that many of you have never believed them," Jed took a long paused as he readied himself for the reaction of the crowd, "It turned out that this girl wasn't a human at all. She was a Lycan."

"Liar!" screamed a few of the people before him, "Lycans are made up creatures!"

"I can assure they are not made up!" Jed called over the roar of voices.

"Silence!" Edgar called loudly and the sound of a drum beat loudly from somewhere behind Jed. The crowd fell silent again.

"Let the boy speak." Edgar ordered.

"I can't believe you're listening to this!" a villager called from the front of the crowd, "You are as mad as the boy!"

"The girl saved my life and also saved my brother's life. A few days ago he was on his death bed after being bitten by a wolf. He would have died if she hadn't saved him and now because of all this she is facing a death sentence. We are here today to try and save her and to try and save the lives of the people who will be lost if this war does not end." Jed called over the murmurs.

"Where is your proof?" One villager shouted. At this Jed turned to look at Ivy and Fang praying that one of them would have the courage to prove all that he'd just said.

He knew how scared they must be to have to face so many humans and know that they might never leave the village walls again. He knew that they must be seeing death in the faces of all the people they looked upon. Relief and hope filled Jed as Fang stepped forward, pulling his arms from the grip of the guards. Within moments he was changing. It happened much quicker than it had in the throne room. Maybe he wanted to make a bigger impact on the people who stood before him. Maybe he wanted to frighten them a little. Maybe he was just growing impatient. But it happened and Jed could see on the faces of the villagers that they were astonished by what they saw. The guards who stood around Fang were pushed out of the way as he grew and changed into the huge black wolf. They scrambled away from him clearly frightened for their lives. Every face began to pale with fear as they stared at the creature that stood before them.

"Kill it!" a loud screech came from the back of the crowd.

"There will be no killing today!" roared Edgar and he gestured for the archers to remain still as they began to look as though they were about to loose arrows into Fang's chest.

"What is wrong with all of you?" a familiar voice suddenly rose up from within the crowd. Jed looked down to see his mother shoving her way to the front of the crowd,

"This creature has not tried to harm any of you and yet you still want his blood." Jed watched in amazement as his mother stepped up onto the stone in front of Jed, "My son trusts this creature and if he does then I do too."

"Liz, what the hell are you playing at?" Jed felt his heart sink as he heard his father's voice. He looked over his mother's shoulder to see that both his father and older brother had followed her to the front.

"I have met Cara, the girl who saved my sons' lives," Liz explained as she turned to address the whole crowd, "She is a brave, strong young woman and if what Jed says is true then she does not deserve to die."

"She's right. None of them deserve to die." Jed called as he took of his mother's shoulder, "The wolves that have been killed aren't really wolves. They aren't mindless beasts. They are a species much more complex and close to humans than we could ever believe. Would you turn on your neighbours right now and pierce their heart with a dagger?" Jed glanced at Ivy seeing her face filled with hope as she stared at the crowd who had turned completely silent for the first time since the hearing had begun, "Would you kill your sons and daughters just because they are a little different? I believe that if given the chance Lycans and humans can live side by side. Who knows maybe we could even hunt together."

The crowd began to look at each other again sounding as though they were considering all that he had said. Before any of them could speak Edgar stepped down beside Jed.

"I believe this boy's heart is true," he explained as he placed a hand on Jed's shoulder much like Jed had done to his mother, "I have decided that I will take a party of guards to the forest and we will talk to the leader of the Lycans." There were sudden protests screeched and shouted from all corners of the square.

"I have heard enough! I have made my decision. Any person who wishes to join the party may do so but no weapons will be held by those who are not guards." With that Edgar turned and began to head back up the steps toward the doors. He took hold of Margret's hand again and began to lead her through the doors. Just over the threshold he turned and looked at Jed and the others,

"Tell my son to return to his human form and you may return to your quarters." Then he disappeared inside the house. Jed turned to see that Fang was already returning to his human form. The relief of no longer seeming to be on trial weakened Jed's knees and he would have fallen if not for his mother's arms wrapping tightly around him.

"Mam, I'm sorry but I have to go." Jed told her as he tried to pull himself away. After a few moments she released him and looked up into his face.

"I understand but you make sure you come home as soon as you can. Keep your brother safe." She ordered. Jed nodded and kissed her quickly on the cheek before turning and leading his friends back up the steps. He wrapped his arm around Jasper's shoulder and led him over the threshold.

"I wish we could go home." Ivy whispered behind him.

"We will be back under the trees before you know it." Fang promised her. Jed looked around to see that he'd wrapped Ivy in his arms and was leading her through the house as though she was a child or maybe even blind.

***

Losing Faith

Cara's stomach growled as she turned over on the rough stone ground of the cave where she'd been imprisoned for the last three days. Outside the sun was dawning on the third day of her imprisonment and she found her hope failing her. For the last few days she'd done nothing but think of Jed and the others as they'd travelled back to the village and how they could be getting on. She had never been one for praying but she had done so many times since she'd been dragged back to the cave. Even though she had no idea who she was praying to her found that it calmed her nerves a little when she felt as though she had someone to talk to. Her hunger and thirst had been fed by small amounts of leftovers from the rest of the pack. She found herself turning her nose up at the half eaten rabbit legs that had been thrown to her but forced herself to eat them knowing she had to keep her strength up. The thought that she might be executed at any time was draining the little store of energy she had left and she began to pray that Jed and the others would return even if the news was bad.

The sound of footsteps approaching through the tunnel entrance of the cave forced her to raise her head. As she lifted it she began to feel dizzy and almost threw up the tiny amount of food that had made it into her stomach. Forcing down the bile she sat up as her mother entered the cave. She knelt down beside her daughter and produced a small cloth pouch from her pocket. Cara looked at the bright blue berries that were hidden within the cloth. She glanced at her mother feeling confused.

"I know it's not meat but it's better than nothing." Her mother explained. Cara smiled weakly as she took the berries from her mother, "I hate to see you like this." Eva sighed as Cara scoffed the berries barely even tasting them. She struggled not to flinch as she felt her mother stroke her hair.

"It doesn't matter. It will be over soon." Cara rasped as she wiped the berry juice from her lips. Her mother looked as though she didn't have a clue what to say.

"They aren't coming back are they?" Cara felt the last of her hope slip away as she saw her mother's hopeless expression.

"That boy of yours just might surprise you." Cara was surprised by the warm tone of voice her mother used as she spoke of Jed, "He seemed determined to save you and anyone who is that determined deserves to win."

"Time's up, Eva." Another pack member called from the entrance of the cave. Eva sighed and took to her feet.

"I'll see if I can get Wren and Luna to gather some more berries for you." She told her daughter as she placed a kiss on her grimy forehead before heading back out of the cave. Cara found herself struggling not to try as she watched her mother go. She had lost all her hope. There was nothing left. Even her mother seemed to be struggling with positive thoughts and that never happened. Her mother was always positive.

She took a deep breath as she collapsed back onto her back. The stone had grown more comfortable as the days passed by loose pebbles still jabbed in her from time to time. The berries her mother had brought had barely taken the edge off her hunger and she longed for the taste of meat as she smelled the scent of deer wafting from the main cave. She could hear the sound of skin tearing as her pack mates enjoyed their breakfast meal and it made her stomach growl even louder. She imagined that everyone in the main cave would be able to hear it. It made her feel fragile and vulnerable. It would take nothing for one of her pack mates to take it upon themselves to execute her before the time was up. She wouldn't be able to put up much of a fight in her weakened state.

No sooner had Eva disappeared than a loud commotion came from the main cave. Cara strained her ears to hear what was going on as she pushed herself back into an awkward sitting position.

"What is the meaning of this?" Alder's commanding voice was just loud enough for Cara to here, "How dare you bring a human into our den?" Cara's heart began to race as she instantly realised who her uncle was talking about. Jed had returned.

With new found hope and energy Cara pushed herself to her feet and without thinking rushed through the tunnel to the main cave. She hit Boulder head first. The man stood like a brick wall blocking the entrance to the tunnel. He barely moved as she collided with him. He didn't even look at her. Instead his eyes were fixed on the group in the middle of the main cave. Peering over Boulder's shoulder Cara saw that Alder was stood towering over Ivy. The ginger haired girl stood bravely gazing up into Alder's eyes. Cara felt her heat warm to see her friend so defiant. She was even more overjoyed when she saw Jed stood behind her. Ivy seemed to be shielding him from the anger in Alder's eyes. What was more disturbing was the way the rest of the pack had begun to circle them. They seemed to be in hunting formation as though they were about to attack. Cara's heart beat quickened until she felt as though she was choking on it.

"You had better have a good explanation for this or you will be joining Cara in the afterlife." Alder snarled revealing pointed fangs.

"Lord Edgar wishes to speak with you. He sent us to take you to him." Ivy explained. Cara could hear the worry in her friend's voice and she felt it too. If Alder refused to meet with Edgar then it would all be over and she would be dead before dawn. She found herself holding her breath as she waited impatiently for her uncle's answer.

"I will not set foot near the village." Alder protested. Cara felt her hope shatter into a thousand tiny pieces. She struggled to control that tears that threatened to cascade down her cheeks. It was all over. She was done for.

"That is why Edgar is waiting in the forest for you." Ivy's words made Cara's heart skip a beat. She was suddenly scared. Could Edgar have set a trap? Was her friend unknowingly leading them to their deaths?

Alder seemed to be thinking. The cave became alive with the hum of chattering. Cara clutched her hands together unable to breathe.

"Bring Cara to me." Alder demanded flicking his wrist in a commanding gesture. Boulder turned and grabbed roughly hold of her. She was too weak to fight against him and she allowed him to half carry her toward her uncle.

"If this is a trap she will be the first to die." Alder explained looking only at Jed. The man nodded and turned to lead the way out of the cave. He glanced at Cara with a frown of worry plastered to his face.

"I'm ok." Cara mimed to him. He seemed to relax a little at this and quickened his pace.

Outside the light was strong. The scent of spring hung in the air. The last of the snow had melted away leaving the earth drenched and slippery. Cara's knees felt weak as she struggled to keep up with the group. Boulder held onto her around her waist, helping her to walk.

They weren't far from the cave when the sound of voices hit Cara's ears. The strong stench of human hit her nostrils before the camp came into view. Around a burned out fire were many figures. They milled around as though waiting for something. On the other side of the clearing stood a large tent of red silky material that was erected with huge wooden poles and tied with long lengths of rope. A guard stood on each side of the entrance to the tent.

As the group entered the camp they were surrounded by guards. Cara saw her pack mates' tense and felt Boulder's grip on her get tighter. Now her feet barely touched the ground as he carried her more than supported her to walk into the tent. Inside the tent was pretty bare. Other than a large wooden table and chairs there was no furniture. Wooden boards had been placed over the muddy ground to ease the effort of walking through sludge. At the table sat two men. Cara guessed that one of them was Edgar though she had no idea which and no clue who the second man was.

"Lord Edgar this is Alder Ironblood, leader of my pack and uncle to Baccara Ironblood." Ivy spoke confidently as she gestured first to her leader and then to Cara.

"Alder, please take a seat." Edgar gestured to the chair opposite him. Alder raised a hand and shook his head.

"I would prefer to stand."

"Then may I offer you a drink?" Edgar asked.

"I would prefer we skip pleasantries and get to the reason we are here." Alder spoke in a tone that was neither cruel nor kind. His expression was a passive one.

Lord Edgar looked taken aback for a moment. He then stood pushing his chair away with the back of his knees which made a horrible noise on the wooden boards below. The sound made Cara grit her teeth.

"Why have you invited me here?" Alder demanded when Lord Edgar remained silent.

"Jedidiah and Edward have told me of your people and explained the hardships you have been through." Edgar explained.

"You mean the hardships your people have put us through?" Alder's voice remained neutral though Cara could see him clenching and unclenching his fists.

"That may be so but we are not here to discuss such matters. We are here to come up with a treaty which will mean the safety of both our people." Edgar explained, "On our journey here Jedidiah told me of the death charge against your niece and why it is so."

"And what is it to you?" Alder demanded.

"I would not like to see such a pretty young thing wasted for saving the lives of not one but two of my villagers." Edgar explained. Cara felt stunned. She hadn't even realised that he'd looked at her enough to determine that she was pretty. It made her skin crawl but she forced herself to remain both still and quiet.

"The judgements I pass within my pack are of no concern of yours." Alder protested. Cara felt as though she was stood on the edge of a cliff just waiting to be pushed over. She could either be pulled back or sent plummeting to her death yet it seemed that her uncle was the one who wanted to do the pushing.

"That may be the case but I would like to come to an agreement with you that may stop this feud between our families." Edgar continued. Alder looked thoughtful.

The silence in the tent was broken as Alder asked,

"What is it that you are suggesting?" Lord Edgar smiled as he prepared to speak yet again. Cara held her breath wondering what conditions the human had come up with and whether her uncle would agree.

"I propose that there be no killing of wolf nor human from this day forward and that human and wolf hunt side by side and work together to achieve a new and better relationship between our village and your pack."

"Why would we hunt with you?" Alder demanded, "You are not fast and you are definitely not skilled hunters." This clearly ruffled Edgar's feathers and Cara could tell he was growing impatient with their conversation.

"In return for your protection on our hunts we will give you half of the kill," Edgar explained, "Wolves are not the only problem we encounter when hunting. There are the bears and mountain lions too." Alder raised a hand and scratched his chin.

"We will hunt with you on one condition." Alder replied.

"Go on." Edgar encouraged.

"No human will come up the mountain and we have a right to protect our den if necessary." Alder raised his chin and shoulders as though he was daring Edgar to object. Cara was relieved when he didn't.

"Then I guess it is settled. There will be no more killing between human and wolf." Edgar rounded the table to stand in front of Alder. He raised a hand and for once Cara knew what the gesture meant. Alder stood looking at Edgar's hand in confusion.

"Shake his hand." Cara told her uncle with the last bit of her strength. Alder lifted his hand and shook Edgar's.

"Does this mean that Cara is free to go?" Ivy asked the question that they had all been itching to hear. Alder glanced at Ivy before turning to look at Cara.

"No." he replied. Cara felt her heart stop. She couldn't determine the expression on her uncle's face but she had a terrible feeling inside her. Her body began to grow cold starting from her fingers and she felt her knees give away beneath her. Before she could fall Jed was by her side. He held on to her as though he was determined not to let her touch the ground.

"Cara you still broke the law while it held and that means you must be punished." Alder explained, "You will spend the next month in solitary confinement while I decide what your punishment will be."

"Isn't that punishment enough?" Jed protested, "Look at her." Cara could hear the pleading in his voice but she knew her uncle would not listen. He shook his head and added,

"I can either rethink your punishment or stick to my earlier decision. The choice is yours."

With that he headed out of the tent taking Boulder with him. Cara looked up at Jed barely able to keep her eyes open. Seeing her parched, dry lips Jed took his water skin from his belt and removed the cork. As soon as he placed it to her lips she began to drink as though she'd never tasted anything so good. The water breathed life back into her as she felt it slide soothingly down her sand paper throat.

"I guess this is the end." Jed whispered to her as he held her in his arms. Cara shook her head,

"This is just the beginning."